Still Alive?

The Alive? Series, Book 2

By: Melissa Woods

Dedicated to Clark. You inspire me to write, to laugh, to love, and to be the best mum I can possibly be. Thank you for being you.

STILL ALIVE?
Copyright ©2019 Melissa Woods
All rights reserved.
Printed in the United States of America
First Edition: June 2019

Clean Teen Publishing
WWW.CLEANTEENPUBLISHING.COM

Summary: Violet has survived a year of the zompocalypse. Now, she's living in a community called Harmony while trying to piece her life back together following the loss of one of her closest friends. But things in Harmony are not always as they seem, and Violet's world—as usual—becomes more complicated than she ever could have anticipated.

ISBN: 978-1-63422-345-4
Cover Design by: Marya Heidel
Typography by: Courtney Knight
Editing by: Cynthia Shepp

COVER ART
© JEFF SCHULTES/FOTOLIA
© KWEST/FOTOLIA
© LIUKOVMAKSYM/FOTOLIA
© NEOSTOCK

Young Adult Fiction /Apocalyptic & Post-Apocalyptic
Young Adult Fiction / Zombies
Young Adult Fiction / Action & Adventure / Survival Stories

For more information about our content disclosure, please utilize the QR code above with your smart phone or visit us at WWW.CLEANTEENPUBLISHING.COM.

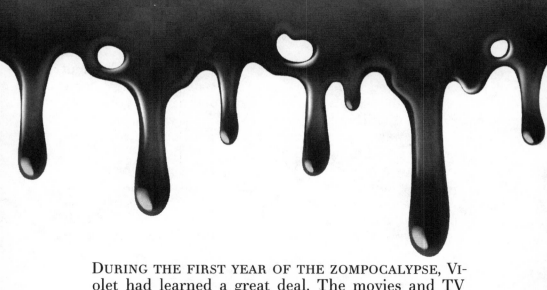

DURING THE FIRST YEAR OF THE ZOMPOCALYPSE, Violet had learned a great deal. The movies and TV shows she used to watch had gotten it wrong. They'd made the living dead look like slow, shambling creatures that could be easily outpaced by a senior citizen taking a brisk stroll. Real zombies were nothing like that. They were as fast as the people they used to be, and they had the advantage of never getting tired. Violet, who used to get out of breath walking downstairs, had been forced to adjust.

ONE

Fast zombies were not the only complication in her life. She had been bitten by one of the undead on the first day, and although she had survived the encounter, she'd developed a rather unusual tick—every time she smelled fresh blood, she became just like the other zombies. It usually lasted until she had fed, at which point she would pass out and wake up in a pool of someone else's blood, feeling more than a little embarrassed about accidentally eating a person.

Another lesson she'd learned was that whenever things seemed to be going well, they weren't. She could be having an awesome day, only to have it crash down around her within the space of a few minutes. That morning, when she found her best friend crouched over a fresh corpse with blood around his mouth, she realized it was going to be one of those days.

1

"Joe..." Violet groaned, stomping into the room and slamming the door. He stood, wiping his lips and swaying a little. Unlike Violet, who had been bitten, Joe had been infected with the virus in a lab using a trial vaccine made from her blood. It had been effective at keeping him from turning into a full zombie after he was bitten. However, he now had the same thirst for human flesh as she did. His infection was slightly different, though—he didn't pass out after feeding. After eating for a while he'd come to, but wouldn't remember much of what had happened.

Less than twenty minutes ago, she'd left him searching a bedroom in the empty house they were looting, only to return to this gruesome scene and his blissfully bewildered expression.

At the sound of her voice, he blinked rapidly.

"This place was empty twenty minutes ago." Violet sighed, running a hand down her messy brown braid. "How did you manage to—"

"Hang on a minute," he interrupted. "This isn't my fault."

She pointed to what was left of the man. "I don't think it was *his*." She paced the room anxiously, panicking as she tried to figure out what to do. The others were almost finished looting the house next door and would be joining them any moment. "We need to cover this up. Fast."

Joe stood awkwardly beside the dead body. "Sorry, Vi."

She softened her tone at his guilty expression. "I know you didn't mean to. Trust me." She'd eaten enough people herself to know it wasn't exactly a conscious choice. "What happened?" she asked.

Joe gestured to the open closet door behind her. "He was hiding in there. When you left, he came out and tried to stab me."

Violet caught sight of the bloodied knife on the ground, only now realizing Joe had a large slash on his shoulder.

"We fought," he continued, "and he got cut."

She didn't need to hear any more. Once the man began to bleed, Joe would have had no control over himself. The hunger was too intense. He would've forgotten everything as he became overwhelmed by the need to feed.

She took a breath, trying to think clearly. In all the time she and Joe had been with their new group, they'd managed to keep the fact they were both infected a secret. They couldn't blow it now. "We need a plan. If the others come in and find him, they'll know something happened."

"Do you think?"

"Okay, your sarcasm is not appreciated right now."

He grinned, always one to make light of situations. "Relax. We've got loads of time."

They were interrupted by the sound of the front door. Violet's eyes widened. Face flushing, Joe hastily grabbed a bedsheet and flung it over the corpse.

"That's it?" she hissed. "That's your plan?"

Joe held up his hands. "I don't know. Maybe I'm not exactly thinking clearly after having just eaten someone!"

Violet could hear footsteps on the stairs. Any second, whoever it was would be in the bedroom. Even if they somehow didn't see the clear shape of a person under the sheet, Joe was covered in blood. The whole thing would raise too many questions.

"Hide," she ordered, forcing Joe under the bed. He resisted a little, but an angry Violet was not one to be tested. Within seconds, he was out of sight.

She hurried across the room. If she met whoever it was in the hallway, they wouldn't even need to come into the bedroom. But as she reached the door, Jack arrived at the top of the stairs.

Tall, with skin the color of cool umber and a smile that reached the corners of his eyes, he met her gaze cheerfully. "Hey, Vi, ready to go?"

"Yep," she answered, her voice much higher than normal. *Let's take it down a notch*, she thought. She sounded way too happy to be looting a house in the land of the dead.

Jack regarded her somewhat curiously. She didn't need a mirror to know she was a mess. Her hair was falling free from her braid, her normally pale face flushed red with anxiety.

His voice was gentle. "Are you okay?"

Violet nodded enthusiastically. "Uh-huh, yeah. Let's

go." She made to walk down the hall, but he pointed over her shoulder.

"What's that?" His eyes were focused on the sheet-covered corpse.

"What?"

Good one, Violet, real casual. There was clearly a body behind her, and acting as though nothing was there was crazy.

Jack raised an eyebrow. "*That* wasn't there earlier."

"Oh, *that*." She smiled. "That's nothing."

"Nothing? It's clearly something. What is it?"

Violet searched for a believable answer, but her head was empty. After flailing for a few moments, she simply said, "That's... that's Joe."

Jack's expression evolved from curiosity to confusion. "Joe?"

It was a ridiculous explanation. There was no reason he'd be under a sheet, but she kept going. "Yeah. He's... napping."

"Under the blanket?"

"Yes."

"With his head covered up?"

"Yes." Violet kept her expression balanced. "That's what he does. It's normal for him."

Skeptically, Jack said, "Right. Okay." He glanced at the blanket once more. "Well, wake him up. We need to go to the last house."

"Will do." She gave a little salute. All it did was make her behavior even more unusual.

Jack paused, a confused smile crossing his lips, then turned and headed down the stairs. Violet felt her heartbeat finally return to normal. She leaned against the wall with a sigh as Joe came out from under the bed, clapping his hands slowly.

"Brilliant. That was so smooth. Why *wouldn't* I be napping in the middle of the floor with a sheet over my face?"

Violet put her hands on her hips. "At least he's gone." She reached into her backpack. Pulling out a bottle of water, she tossed it to him. "Clean your face off, then we need to leave."

THEY'D BEEN WORKING THEIR WAY THROUGH THIS STREET for the past few days, clearing each house one at a time. Everything that could be used was taken and loaded into the truck. That was Violet's life now. She was a scavenger.

"Can't we think of a nicer name?" she'd asked Jack upon hearing their job title for the first time. "Calling us 'scavengers' makes us sound—"

"Like thieves who rummage through dead people's stuff?" Joe suggested.

"That's what we do," Jack had replied.

And so, the name stuck. Violet tried not to think about it too much, but it wasn't exactly something she planned to put on her gravestone: Violet Winter—friend, daughter, half-zombie, collector of dead people's crap.

"Just one left," Joe said as they headed to the house at the end of the road. It was three stories with an overgrown front yard and a few broken windows. An abandoned tricycle in the grass was nearly swallowed by weeds. This wasn't an unusual scene. Wear and tear came part and parcel with the new world. When everyone spent their days running from the dead, things like gardening and painting the fence tended to take a backseat. It had been a year since the outbreak, long enough for nature to begin reclaiming what it wanted.

Violet surveyed the building as Joe zipped up his jacket at her side. The blood had been wiped away from his mouth, though his pupils were still mildly dilated. She hoped it wasn't enough for the others to notice.

Other than the part-time zombism, Joe was relatively unchanged from a year ago. Still tall and skinny, with brown hair and—thanks to the virus—grey eyes. His skin, like Violet's, had also lightened, which made it seem like they hadn't seen sunlight in weeks. Lately, they were often mistaken for brother and sister.

The most noticeable change about Joe was the mustache. He'd been working on it for the past few months. Although it made him look like he belonged in an eighties' cop drama, Violet didn't quite have the heart to tell him because he was so proud of it.

"Let's hope for some good stuff," he muttered. "What could possibly go wrong?" He, threw her a wink at this horror cliché.

"Does everyone know what they need?" Jack asked. He, Lex, and Connie had parked the truck directly outside the house.

Jack surveyed each of the scavengers in turn. At twenty-two, he was a few years older, but he could easily pass for thirty. His face was stubbled, his dark eyes suggesting he'd seen more than twenty years would allow. His arms were scarred, as was his right cheek, but Jack was a survivor. Violet had never seen him so much as pause when there was work to be done. He was one of Ezra's soldiers, there to keep them safe while they did their job. That was part of the deal. Without an escort, they weren't allowed to scavenge. It was for their protection.

"We should go through it again," he said.

Lex, seventeen, with russet skin and a black mohawk, rolled her eyes in frustration. "We know. It's the same stuff we've needed for the past week. You don't have to do this every time."

"This has to be smooth. We've only got a few hours until we have to get back."

Lex reeled off the items in a flat tone. "Medicine, food, batteries."

"Books for the children," Connie added, her watery blue eyes darting nervously around the empty street. She reminded Violet of a mouse—small, pale, and always acting as though a predator was around every corner. She wasn't exactly wrong.

"Weapons," Joe said.

Violet could do with something new. She had a crowbar, which was useful, but what she really wanted was a machete. She'd seen a few soldiers and scavengers with them, and they were perfect zombie killers.

"We need clothes as well," she added.

Jack nodded. "Okay, let's go." He headed down the path first, swinging his baseball bat casually as he walked.

Jack always moved with confidence, as if nothing could ever go wrong. Violet knew he couldn't genuinely believe that. He'd lost people just like she had, but it seemed to have no impact on his attitude. Connie kept close behind him. She had virtually zero weapon skills, holding her own baseball bat as though it were a bomb that might explode. Lex, in contrast, loved to smash biters. Her bloodied axe summed up that picture, as did the 'I kill zombies' tattoo on her left arm.

Joe turned and held out his arm to Violet as if inviting her to walk the promenade with him, then spoke in a clipped, old-fashioned tone. "Shall we, milady?"

"Love to," she said with a smile, but a sense of unease settled in the pit of her stomach, and she couldn't get her legs to move. Nervousness was a given before heading into a new place, but this was something else. She had a bad feeling about this one.

"You okay?" Joe asked, his voice back to normal.

She bit her lip, unable to shake her doubt. "Yeah, I just... I don't know. Something feels wrong."

Joe leaned on his crowbar. "I can't imagine what. Here we are, heading into an unknown building in a world populated by walking, flesh-eating corpses, with nothing for protection but a couple of crowbars... Nothing unusual or worrying there."

Violet smiled. "Yeah, I'm sure it's nothing."

They made their way to the door, where the others were gathered. "Just remember," Joe said, "if anything goes wrong—"

"I know, you've got my back."

He shrugged. "I was going to say we don't need to outrun the biters, just those guys, but sure."

With his bat, Jack knocked on the front door. It was better to draw the biters to the front of the house, so they could see how many were there before they decided to go in. So far on this street, they'd only encountered a couple, which had been taken out without any problems.

There was no movement from inside, so Jack took the crowbar from Violet and quickly wrenched the door open before tossing the weapon back to her. She missed the catch, and it clattered heavily to the ground.

"Nice one." Joe grinned, and she elbowed him in the ribs.

The house was dark and coated in a thick layer of dust. Once inside, Jack gathered his team, Lex and Connie, and went one way. Violet and Joe went the other, heading to the stairs. They stopped at the bottom.

"A pack of gum says they creak," Joe whispered. Violet shook his hand, then tentatively put her foot on the first step. No noise.

"Pay up," she hissed.

"Got to make it all the way to the top—that's the bet."

She continued, the thick dust muffling her footsteps on the wooden floorboards. The last step let out a loud creak.

Joe grinned victoriously. "Told you. They always creak. It's such a cliché."

Violet reached into her pocket, pulling out her precious last pack of gum and thrusting it at his chest.

She and Joe checked the rooms on their level. All were clear of both the dead and the living, which Violet was grateful for. She didn't trust other survivors, having had too many bad experiences with new people.

They moved to the third floor, clearing most of it quickly, until there was only one room left. Violet reached for the door handle.

"Wait," Joe interrupted. "This is the only room with a closed door. I bet there's something awful in there."

"I can't bet. I don't have any more gum."

"You've got that candy bar you've been saving."

"Okay, you're on." She stepped back, gesturing for him to open the door. It creaked open, and he peered inside.

"Pay up," he muttered.

Violet gripped her crowbar more tightly as she followed him into the room, but there were no zombies. It was just a regular bedroom, probably a teenage boy's, with posters on the walls, a pile of dirty dishes on the desk, and crumpled clothes on the floor. She raised a brow. "I thought you said there'd be something awful in here?"

"There is." Joe pointed to a poster by the window, of a

child pop star whose name Violet couldn't remember.

She snorted. "That doesn't count."

"Name one good thing he's ever done."

"Well... Give me a minute."

"Exactly." Joe went over to the door. "Clear up here," he yelled before putting his backpack on the floor and taking out a roll of trash bags. He tore one off, tossed the roll to her, then started opening the dresser drawers and stuffing his bag full of clothes.

"I'll get the medicine," Violet said, heading to the bathroom on the floor below. Lex was already there.

"Hey," Lex muttered, dropping a few boxes of pills into her bag.

"Anything good?"

She shook her head. "A few painkillers, no antibiotics. Still, we'll take everything." She reached for a box at the back of the medicine cabinet, examined it, and smiled. She shook it at Violet. "You want these?"

They were birth control pills. Violet raised an eyebrow. "What would I need those for?"

"If I have to explain what they're for, then you don't need them." She lowered her voice. "I thought you and Joe were—"

"No," Violet interrupted. "We're just friends. That's all we've ever been."

Lex shrugged, dropping the pills into her bag. "Not a lot of options these days."

"I'm going to check one of the other bathrooms," Violet said, turning back to the hallway. In reality, she just wanted to get away from the conversation. It made her feel weird and uncomfortable. Lex seemed to enjoy making people feel awkward—it was her idea of fun. Violet liked the girl, but she still couldn't quite read her.

As Violet headed down the hallway, Jack called her name. She peeked through a door to see he'd filled two trash bags already.

"You want these?" He held out a pair of women's sunglasses. They looked expensive, not that that meant anything these days.

She took them and tried them on. "What do you

9

think?"

"Fantastic. You're a vision."

She grinned, posing as though he were taking a picture. Jack was much friendlier than their last escort. Over the past few months, they'd become friends.

"Joe's packing clothes upstairs, too," she said.

"That's good. Do you know if Lex found any medicine?"

"A few things. No antibiotics."

"We'll keep looking. It needs to be a priority." His tone was serious, but he didn't seem worried. Violet liked that. He made her feel calmer, and she'd needed that over the past nine months. Ever since—

Don't think about it, not now, not here, she admonished herself.

"What's wrong?" Jack asked, taking a step toward her, his expression concerned.

Violet backed up "Nothing. I'm going to see what Joe's doing." She stumbled in her haste to get out of the room, hurrying up the stairs. That had been too close. She wasn't ready to talk about her feelings, not with anyone. Over the past few months, she'd developed a new rule to live by— *don't let anyone get too close.* It was safer for everyone that way.

She found Joe sprawled out on an unmade bed.

"Working hard?" she asked sarcastically. He patted the space beside him without opening his eyes. She put the sunglasses into one of the bags, then dropped on her back beside him.

"I used to have a room like this," he murmured.

"*Just* like this?" She flicked her gaze to the clothes on the floor and the moldy plates on the desk.

"Oh, yeah."

"Real bachelor pad?"

"Girls couldn't resist."

"Did you have dirty underwear hanging off the door handle, too?"

"Violet, I had it hanging everywhere. That was the vibe of the room."

She snorted. "Those lucky ladies."

Neither spoke for a few moments until she leaned up

on her elbows. "Doesn't it feel weird? A year ago, this was normal life. Just lying on a bed, doing nothing at all."

"Hey, what makes you think I did 'nothing at all' with the girls on my bed?"

"Just a guess."

He grinned. "Sam was always the one who brought girls home." His face fell, the way it always did when he spoke about his best friend and roommate. They'd survived several months of the zompocalypse together before Sam was killed. He'd been injected with a different prototype vaccine and not survived the process. Joe didn't talk about him often. They didn't talk about any of the people they had lost.

From somewhere outside, Jack said, "I'm going into the attic. There might be stuff up there."

"Okay," Violet replied, making no attempt to move.

"Oh, I forgot. I found this for you." Joe reached behind him, then held up a slightly squashed candy bar.

Her eyes widened. "Is that a Chunko?"

"Yep, and that's the worst name for a chocolate bar ever."

"Give it to me!"

Violet felt almost giddy when he handed it to her. Sure, she had no sense of taste since becoming a half-zombie, but this had always been her favorite candy and was worthy of celebration whether she could taste it or not.

"This is the best day ever." She grinned, pocketing her prize. *Wait a minute,* she thought. *Things never go this well. Something is—*

"Guys!"

Violet and Joe were at the bedroom door in a matter of seconds. Jack had practically fallen down the attic ladder and was now frantically trying to push it back up. Unfortunately, the five zombies leaning through the hole were interfering with his plan.

"Just go," Joe yelled, pushing Jack away from the ladder. The three of them charged for the stairs as the sounds of falling zombies followed them.

"Get out!" Jack called as they ran.

Lex appeared, throwing her backpack on, eyes flicking to the stairs. Violet studied her face, knowing Lex's reaction would show how serious the situation was.

Lex's eyes widened, and she began to run.

Okay, that means a lot of zombies.

They made it to the second set of stairs just as the screaming started.

"Connie," Jack gasped as they ground to a halt.

She appeared below them, clutching her bleeding neck, stumbling up the first few steps. Four biters came from behind and were upon her in moments. Now the group was trapped; they couldn't go down, but the biters from the attic would reach them in seconds.

"In here," Lex ordered, motioning to a bedroom to their left. They all bundled inside, and Jack slammed the door shut just as the zombies from the attic began to hammer their rotten hands upon it. The guys held it closed while Violet and Lex searched for something heavy enough to block it.

"Help me move this," Lex called, grabbing hold of one end of a large wooden armoire. Violet tried to help drag it across the room, but it was too heavy.

"Help them," Joe said. "I can hold it."

Jack looked unsure but hurried over to help. Finally, they positioned the armoire against the door. It kept it shut. For now, at least.

Violet felt beads of sweat on her forehead and wiped them away roughly with her sleeve. Joe was panting from exertion. When she put her hand on his back, he gave her a weak smile.

"Connie..." Jack sighed, eyes on the floor.

"She shouldn't have come," Lex said, shaking her head. "She wasn't meant for this."

Jack pointed to the door. "She came to help."

"And got herself killed. I told you she wasn't strong enough," Lex said.

He glared at her.

"How are we going to get out of here?" Violet asked as the sounds from outside the room got louder. It seemed the biters from downstairs were now joining the others. Food was in the bedroom, and they knew it.

"Come on," Lex said, her tone almost bored. "You know I never do anything without a reason." She moved to the window, opening it and climbing onto the sloped roof. At the edge, she lowered herself before dropping quietly onto the ground below.

"I hate when she's right," Jack muttered, following her lead. Violet and Joe did the same.

Back on the ground, Jack and Lex began arguing again.

"We have to," he insisted.

"It's a waste of time." Lex's tone was exasperated.

"We're not discussing this. I'm going back in." He headed to the front of the house, removing his knife from his back pocket as he went. This, Violet knew, was rule one. Ezra hadn't made many rules when he founded their community, but the first was to put anyone bitten out of their misery before they turned. It was one of the reasons Violet had agreed to join the group, since it was a philosophy she could get on board with.

"Why don't you want him to do it?" she asked Lex. "We all agreed."

"We promised to do it as long as it doesn't put survivors in danger," Lex corrected, watching Jack disappear into the house. "You're telling me him going back in there doesn't put *him* in danger?"

She had a point, but Jack needed to end Connie's suffering. It was the right thing to do.

"He's quiet and experienced. I'm sure he'll be—" Unfortunately, Violet was interrupted by Jack's reappearance as he charged out of the house and ran at full speed toward the truck. He was followed closely by the biters.

"Maybe finish that later." Joe sighed, pulling Violet away as the sounds of feet pounding on concrete drew ever closer.

THEY MANAGED TO GET INTO THE TRUCK BEFORE anyone else got bitten, and Jack began the drive back home.

Violet was glad they'd at least had their scavenged finds from the other house loaded, but had hoped for more. She wondered how Lex and Joe were faring in the back of the truck. It was usually a rough ride, particularly if they'd gotten a big haul. That wasn't an issue today, though.

She drummed her fingers against the door, the cool breeze from the open window soothing on her face. The last few weeks had been uncomfortably hot. She desperately wanted to roll up the long sleeves of her shirt but had no choice but to keep them down. Jack, like almost everyone else she knew, had no idea she'd been infected with the zombie virus. Unlike Joe's bite, which was easily hidden on his shoulder, hers was on her lower left arm.

Sometimes she wondered what Jack would do if he saw it. Would he kill her immediately? It was, after all, rule one. Violet doubted she'd have time to explain herself before the soldier did his job, whether he was her friend or not. So, she kept it hidden, kept the secret, and coped with the unpleasantries it caused.

Jack, usually a talker, silently watched the road

T
W
O

ahead. She knew he felt bad about Connie. She did, too, although her emotions were less cut and dried. Her guilt was about not being able to help, rather than being upset someone had died. These days, the deaths of those around her didn't seem to resonate as much. Joe would be different, Violet assumed, since he was like a brother to her, but most other losses barely caused a hint of emotion. Most of the time, she was simply happy not to have been the one who killed them.

Jack tapped his fingers against the steering wheel. "We'll go out again tomorrow."

Violet nodded. They'd have to. Ezra didn't take failure lightly. Or so she'd heard. He wasn't a cruel man, but he had an air about him that made everyone stand up a little straighter and work a little harder to keep him happy. No one wanted to be the one to let him down.

They continued the journey in silence, making it back home in good time. The closed gates loomed ahead. There were almost certainly several guns pointed at the truck right now. That was protocol—view all arrivals as potential threats until proven otherwise.

The gates were reinforced sheet metal, which had to be pulled open by a man on each side. They were the only way in or out of Harmony, which was surrounded by a reinforced steel wall about twelve feet high. It was made stronger by metal braces, all of which had been placed on the inside instead of the outside to discourage intruders.

"When people come here, it's because we choose to invite them," Ezra had said. "Not because they climbed in like rats."

The heavy gates began to open. Jack drove in, and they rattled closed again. Everything ran efficiently. Harmony was built on the idea of being completely safe and secure. It was what had brought Violet there in the first place.

Harmony had been built on an expansive patch of land. Before the rise of the dead, it had been in the final stages of a massive construction project. It contained two warehouses, twelve small apartment buildings, and a lot of building materials. The land had previously been overgrown with shrubbery and trees, most of which had been cut down and used, though a few still dotted the landscape. Over the past year, flowers and colorful weeds had sprouted, something the residents encouraged. It made the place feel more like a town.

The biggest warehouse, set against the north wall, was the main hub. The communal dining area and indoor market were downstairs, while Ezra lived upstairs. Violet had no idea what was up there. She, like ninety-nine percent of Harmony's residents, had never been allowed entrance into their leader's private quarters.

Next to the main warehouse was a smaller one, home to soldiers and the medical facility. That was where Jack lived. The three-story apartment buildings scattered around the compound were modest in size, initially designed to supply cheap living for low-income families, and now housed the rest of the survivors.

Some were nicer than others. Where a resident lived was determined by their standing in the community and the points they earned. The three buildings that had been completed and furnished were on the west side. To the east were three slightly smaller ones that were completed but only partially furnished. That was where Violet and the other scavengers lived, being mid-range point holders.

The six buildings in front of the open space known as the 'courtyard' were the shabbiest. Their windows had no glass, and the floors were concrete and plywood. The farmers, traders, and kitchen staff who lived in them worked hard to make their homes more comfortable and secure.

The very lowest point holders lived on the south-east side of the community, in an area affectionately known as The Shacks. It consisted of a mishmash of crooked wooden structures, trailers, and tents. The residents there had few skills to offer and were mostly elderly, infirm, or orphaned children. They survived by either taking on the worst jobs for the fewest points or relying on the kindness of others.

It was late afternoon—earlier than the scavengers would normally return. Disappointed eyes watched the truck. It was obvious they knew the run hadn't been a success. Still, a small crowd began gathering the moment Jack parked. He sighed and climbed out, followed by Violet. She moved around to let the others out of the back. Lex took one look at the faces watching them and disappeared. She hated dealing with people.

The people too low on points to buy anything decent at the markets made up the waiting group, each hoping to strike a deal outside of the system. It was against the rules, but Jack sometimes took pity on them. A can of soup for the man with the walking stick, a toy for one of the kids—items that wouldn't be missed but would make a difference to those people.

They were already haggling, holding up bits of cloth or homemade weapons they thought might be worth something. A young woman with dark red hair tried to drape herself over Jack and whisper in his ear, but he shook his head.

"Sorry, we couldn't get much today. This all goes inside."

There were disgruntled groans, but no one put up much of a fight. The scavengers took their meager supplies to the warehouse market. It didn't take long. They told the market overseer, a skinny man with a sharp face, what they had collected, and he assigned their wages. The limited haul earned Violet only two points for her day's work. That wouldn't usually be enough to live on, but she had twenty saved up.

As they were leaving the warehouse, the bells began to ring. Violet, Jack, and Joe stopped instinctively, and headed to the courtyard. When the bells rang, the community members went to the stage to hear announcements. Attendance was non-negotiable.

"I love these things," Joe drawled, trudging along beside Violet.

She shrugged, "At least Ezra keeps them short."

They joined the crowd surrounding the stage, and everyone fell silent.

Ezra stepped onto the platform. At first glance, he was an ordinary guy in his forties. Average height, strong but not overly muscular, with deep brown hair and eyes. His teeth were incredibly white, and Violet sometimes wondered if he had a bulk supply of whitening strips stashed somewhere. His clothes were always well fitted and immaculate, as evidenced that afternoon by his clean black jeans and a dark blue shirt.

He looked good, but not necessarily like a leader. However, within moments of appearing, it became clear why Ezra was so respected. It wasn't just that he controlled the soldiers. Ezra had something about him that made people want to listen. He was charming, though Violet had never admitted that aloud, but also a little frightening. She had no reason to fear him, but whenever they gathered like this, she couldn't help but feel like a mouse in the presence of a large cat.

"Friends," Ezra began, "today marks the one-year anniversary of when it all went to hell."

Violet hadn't realized that. An entire year of running from zombies. An entire year since she'd gotten bitten. It wasn't exactly an anniversary she'd hurry to celebrate.

Ezra continued. "A few weeks after the dead rose up, the first of us found this place. It began as a random assortment of crappy, half-finished buildings, and look at it now!" He held his arms out, allowing the people to marvel at the beauty of their surroundings.

Violet glanced around. *Oh, there's a woman vomiting over there. And is that man eating a rat on a stick? Lovely.*

"When we built Harmony, it was just me and five of my soldiers."

Internally, she scoffed. They hadn't been real soldiers—just lucky enough to find guns.

"Over the months, as more of you joined us, we created something worthwhile. We became a community. We rebuilt civilization within these walls, and we are *thriving.*"

Violet thought the woman still vomiting by the oak tree undermined his point a bit, but Ezra either didn't see her or pretended not to. He was too absorbed in his speech.

"Life isn't easy here. You work for points, and you earn your keep. We're all born equal, but you must earn your position in this place. Work hard, and you can achieve anything." He grinned, showing his perfect, white teeth. "To celebrate the anniversary of our home, all points will be doubled for the next week!"

There was a cheer and a round of applause from the crowd. Ezra nodded before stepping off the platform and heading toward the warehouse. He was followed by two of his soldiers.

"Double points," Joe muttered. "Lucky, lucky us."

"It's better than nothing."

"I doubt it. The traders will just raise their prices."

"Well, aren't you just a delightful ray of sunshine?" Violet joked. "Come on, let's go home."

THEIR PLACE WAS ON THE SECOND FLOOR OF THE MIDDLE apartment building. Although it didn't look like much, the windows had glass and the door locked. It could've been much worse. As Violet headed up the stairs, she was immediately pounced on by Ben, the small dog she'd found at the start of the zompocalypse. She stroked his white fur. "Hi, boy."

"He's missed you."

Toby smiled at her from the top of the stairs. The ten-year-old was still a foot shorter than she was, but he'd grown a lot over the past few months. Ezra didn't like sending kids out to scavenge, but they were occasionally allowed to take him along as part of his 'training.' When he wasn't doing that, he did what most of the kids did—odd jobs for points. They painted walls, helped harvest the crops, and did anything else the adults didn't want to. It wasn't the hardest work, just monotonous.

"You're back early," Toby said. "Overrun?"

Violet continued up the stairs. "They were in the attic. I guess they were hiding from the dead. One of them must've kept their bite a secret."

"Did anyone—"

"Connie."

Toby nodded, taking the news in stride. "I'll get you

something to eat." He went in through their front door, which led into the kitchen. Violet and Joe followed him into the small room. The building had power most of the time, so there was a fridge—almost always empty—a small stove, and a table with four chairs. Excluding the bathroom, there were four other rooms in their apartment, shared between the seven people who lived there.

Well, six now that Connie was dead.

Two other scavengers were already there. Ella and Ryan were examining something at the table, and Joe dropped into the chair beside them.

"We... are... done!" Ryan grinned triumphantly.

"What?" Joe asked. Violet stepped farther into the room, trying to see what Ryan was holding. It was a baseball bat, but with blades hammered into the sides.

"What is that?" she asked.

Ryan held the bat up, turning it slowly. "It's a bachete!"

"A what?"

"A bat and a machete," Ella explained, gazing at Ryan proudly. "He's been working on it all day."

Ella, a beautiful blonde with sparkling blue eyes, always regarded Ryan as though he were the most interesting creature she'd ever met. Violet supposed he was attractive enough—muscular, with thick, curly brown hair and intense hazel eyes—but probably not the kind of guy Ella would've gone for in the pre-zombie world. Still, she always hung on his every word, and it was mildly amusing how oblivious he was to it.

"Isn't it amazing?" Ryan asked, eyes only for the weapon in front of him.

Joe sighed, running his hand through his hair. "Well, as long as we're not wasting our lives," he said before snatching a slice of apple from the plate Toby handed Violet. She took one herself, chewing absentmindedly. Eating wasn't particularly enjoyable anymore, not since everything had lost its taste. While some aspects of Joe's zombism differed from hers, he'd lost that sense, too, and he also chewed as if it were cardboard.

"It's just gonna be so smooth," Ryan said with a smile, still admiring the bachete.

"Definitely," Ella agreed.

"Think of how many biters I can take out with this."

"You'll be unstoppable."

Violet let her eyes sweep the dingy kitchen. A sudden, intense feeling of being trapped washed over her, which was ridiculous. They weren't prisoners. She, Joe, and Toby could leave if they really wanted. But it wasn't like they had anywhere to go. They hadn't been doing great on their own before. At least here, they were safe. They had jobs, a home, and friends. It just felt like something was missing.

She knew what, even though she never let herself think about it.

They all stayed in the kitchen for a while before heading down to the dining hall, where they met up with Lex and Jack. After filling their trays with as much as they could get for the two points they'd each decided to spend, they went to sit down.

Violet studied her meal. It wasn't too bad today—unidentifiable meat she'd rather not ask about, carrots and peas, and an apple. A quick scan of the room told her she'd made out better than most. Dinner was quick, without much talking. Spirits were still low over their limited haul and the loss of one of their own.

After, the group headed home. It was early, but Violet decided to go to bed, declining the invitation to play cards. In her room, she switched on the small lamp, illuminating the space with a warm yellow light. The bedroom was small but cozy enough with two beds, a closet, a desk, and a bookcase that held a couple of books she'd managed to get for relatively cheap at the markets. The wall behind her bed was her favorite part, though. It was covered almost entirely in photographs.

When they first arrived at Harmony, Violet had found an old instant camera on a supply run. She took a few pictures before the film ran out but struck gold when they'd found boxes of the stuff at a scavenged house. Anything that made her smile was apt to get photographed. Joe was there a lot, pulling faces, posing dramatically, or occasionally caught unaware while reading, laughing, or talking.

There were loads of Toby and Ben and the four of them together. A few other people had made the cut, but Violet didn't really form attachments anymore, so there weren't many of those. Sunsets and flowers were the subjects of most of the other photographs, though there were also a couple of her sleeping, which Joe had taken to creep her out. Whenever a new one appeared on the wall, he'd always pull a confused face and pretend he had no idea how it had gotten there.

Unfortunately, she'd used the last box of film and had yet to find more. There were blank spaces on the wall she was desperate to fill up, but she wasn't feeling particularly hopeful.

Violet lay on her bed. Rolling up the sleeve of her shirt, she ran her finger along the healed bite. She still remembered how it'd felt when the zombie, a woman in a white nightdress, had sunk her teeth deep into the skin. Violet had thought she was safe, having outrun the biters outside and sought refuge in a house. She'd managed to secure the door against the creature that had been chasing her and had taken just a moment to breathe, closing her eyes and trying to come to terms with the horrors she'd seen in the hour since waking up. That moment was all it had taken for a different zombie to find and bite her. A couple of seconds and her life was changed forever. For some reason, unlike anyone else she'd ever come across who'd been bitten, Violet hadn't died. Things were different, but she was still breathing. The scar was black and ugly, but trailing her finger along it always brought comfort. Perhaps because it reminded her that she was still alive.

Today, she needed that. She'd been feeling weird since she woke up. Mostly, she carried on with her life as though nothing had happened. But other times it felt like something had been ripped out of her chest and she was just stumbling along without it. She wanted to sleep, to try to escape the feeling, but when she did that, she dreamed of *him.*

She never said his name anymore. Never even allowed herself to think it. Maybe that made it worse. If she talked about him, it might help. She didn't think so, though. Joe must've shared that view, because he never spoke about him, either. Neither did Toby. They continued as though he had never existed. Violet wondered if he haunted them the same way he haunted her. She doubted it. It wasn't their fault he was dead.

"We need to go!"

"No!" Violet screamed, fighting against the arms pulling her away, dragging her forcefully to the door.

"He's gone!"

Violet knew they were right. She'd seen him fall. But she wouldn't believe it. She couldn't. He couldn't die. He was the one who made the plans, who held everything together. He was the one who kept her safe.

"No!" she screamed again, but she was losing strength now. They had almost pulled her to the door. She could see the biters' bloodied mouths. They'd already finished with him. Now they wanted something fresh.

"Violet, we need to go." Joe's voice. Distant. Weak.

"No..." Violet breathed. But she let him take her.

When Violet woke up, she had blood pouring from her eyes. This was what happened when she cried now. The room was dark. Her forehead was slick with sweat, and she clapped a hand over her mouth to try to calm her choking sobs. Joe stirred at the sound. He climbed out of his own bed and moved over to hers, sliding in beside her and pulling the blanket over them both. His hair was mussed from sleep, but he was already wide awake. The moonlight through the window illuminated his face. Without having to ask, he understood what was happening.

"It's okay," he soothed, putting his arm around her. She shook. The nightmares wouldn't leave, and no matter how tightly Joe held her, she couldn't get warm.

"I dreamt about it again," she sobbed, her breath catching in her throat.

"I know."

"I can't... it won't stop."

He rested her head on his shoulder. "I know. I see it every night, too."

The tears, which Violet thought she had managed to stem, began to flow once more. Slowly, Joe's shirt was covered in splotches of blood. He didn't say anything, though. He just held her as she cried.

"WAKE UP."

Violet almost jumped out of her skin. She could feel the weight of someone straddling her, but all she could see were a pair of brown eyes staring into her own. Without pausing to think, she swung out with the knife kept under her pillow. Luckily, Lex leaned back in time, catching Violet's arm mid-air. She grinned.

"A little paranoid, aren't we?"

"We live in a world full of zombies. There's no such thing as being paranoid anymore."

Lex shrugged, making no attempt to move. "Good point. Feeling better?"

"What do you mean?"

"You were screaming and crying and being weird last night."

Tactful. Thanks, Lex.

"Sorry. I had a nightmare."

"*Children* have nightmares. *You* flipped out."

"Well, I'm fine."

Lex still made no attempt to move, cocking her head to one side. "What was it about?"

"I really don't want to talk about it."

"That's boring."

Violet shifted uncomfortably. "Are you going to get up at any point?"

"Why?"

Before she could answer, the bedroom door opened. Joe entered, a towel around his waist and hair still wet from the shower. He raised an eyebrow at the pair of them. "Morning?"

"Hi Joe," Lex said casually. "You need to hurry up. We're leaving in fifteen minutes." She glanced down at Violet. "You too."

"Then get off me."

She grinned, finally climbing to her feet and striding purposefully out of the room. Joe swung the door shut behind her with one hand.

"She's fun," he said sarcastically, heading to the closet as Violet sat up. He tossed some clothes in her direction, and she quickly got changed.

Sharing a room with a guy might've been awkward before, but after spending a year running from the dead, Violet found herself far less self-conscious. Joe had probably seen her in her underwear more times than she could count, but in her mind, he didn't really qualify as a 'man' anymore, he was just Joe. Turning their backs when getting dressed was the extent of the privacy they gave each other.

Violet pulled on a clean shirt, a thin grey sweater, and a pair of jeans. They were old and torn, and as she sat down, she noticed the seam at the crotch was wearing away.

Great.

She pulled at the seam, unintentionally creating a small hole, then accidentally caught her finger in the material and made it bigger. She groaned, swearing under her breath.

"We should just have sex and get rid of all this tension," Joe said casually. "Seeing you there, ripping the crotch of those old jeans and swearing, is way too much for any guy to handle."

Violet snorted in response.

He held his hand to his heart. "Stop doing that—you know how much I love it when you snort."

She threw her jacket at him. "Come on, let's go."

OUTSIDE, RYAN, LEX, AND ELLA WERE TOSSING THEIR backpacks into the truck. Jack appeared, smiling widely.

"Morning." His white breath cut through the surprisingly cool air.

"Why so chipper?" Lex asked suspiciously.

"I've got a good feeling about today. The place we're going should be full of supplies." His expression wavered as he spotted something over Violet's shoulder. She turned. Ezra and two of his soldiers were approaching.

"Morning gang," Ezra said cheerfully, eyes sweeping across the group. Violet felt uneasy. She'd only ever spoken directly to him once, after first arriving in Harmony. Luckily, he seemed far more interested in Ryan's new weapon than in talking to her.

"That is just beautiful," he said, exhaling. "You think you can teach some of my guys how to make those? There will be points in it for you."

Ryan beamed. "Oh, yeah, absolutely."

Ezra flashed his winning teeth once more. "Excellent." He turned to Jack, his voice suddenly less jovial. "Need a good run today. Don't let me down."

Violet knew 'Don't let me down' actually meant 'You let me down yesterday; doing it again will be bad for you.'

Jack nodded, and Ezra clapped him on the shoulder before heading off in the opposite direction. As soon as he was out of earshot, Jack noticeably relaxed.

"Shall we go?"

He, Violet, and Joe climbed into the front of truck, while Lex and the others took a car, following closely behind.

"I have a good feeling about today," Jack insisted, though Violet couldn't help but think he sounded slightly less sincere than he had a few minutes ago.

"A SWIMMING POOL?"

Violet surveyed the parking lot. Above the glass double doors of the large building was a sign which read 'Sea Foam Swimming Pool'.

Jack, sitting in the driver's seat next to her, smiled. "Yeah, it's perfect."

"All the towels and nose clips we could ever want," Joe drawled.

Violet grinned, but Jack rolled his eyes impatiently.

"No, this place used to have a group living inside. Ezra heard they had loads of supplies, food, medicine, you name it. Enough to keep us going for weeks."

"They're not here anymore?" Violet asked. "Because we don't steal from the living..."

"No, we got lucky—they all died. Some horrible flu thing. Swept through the place and killed them all."

Joe's face was deadpan. "Wow, that *is* lucky."

Jack looked a little sheepish. "I just mean we could do with the supplies, and apparently they're still sitting there. This place could be a gold mine."

"Or it could be a dark nightmare full of wet zombies."

Jack shrugged. "Well, let's find out." He got out of the truck, heading toward the building as confidently as always.

Joe groaned. "I hate how cheerful he always is."

He and Violet followed Jack to the glass doors, where Lex, Ella and Ryan were already waiting. Lex turned as they approached.

"I knocked, but I don't think there's anyone home."

Jack nodded. "Okay, the place is set across two floors. The ground floor has the swimming pool and the café, as well as a couple of offices. The basement has the gym and some big rooms for holding events. We'll check the whole place first, then search for supplies. Who wants what?"

"Violet and I will take the pool and the café," Joe answered. "I don't love the idea of exploring the basement."

Jack thought for a moment. "Take Lex with you. Ella, Ryan, and I will check the basement."

"Awesome," Ryan muttered.

Jack reached for the metal handle and turned it. The door opened noiselessly. Violet had expected it to be locked. Jack paused, and she knew he was thinking the exact same thing she was.

If we can get in this easily, so can anyone else.

But when he turned back to face them, his expression was set. "Let's go."

The group moved inside. Though there was no power, the glass doors and large windows allowed in enough light that they didn't have to use their flashlights. Directly ahead of them was a desk with a cash register and a turnstile. The sign on the wall told them the pool was along the corridor to the right, while the café and stairs to the gym were on the left. The group split in two, and Joe headed to the right.

"Let's check out the pool first," he suggested. He walked through the turnstile and winced as the mechanism made a loud, metallic noise. He froze halfway, the sound echoing off the walls.

"I forgot how loud these things are," he whispered.

"Clearly," Lex hissed.

Violet held onto her crowbar tightly, though she didn't hear the telltale sounds of biters yet. "It would be super great if you didn't make loads of noise," she muttered.

Joe shrugged. "I'm halfway now, let's just rip off the Band-Aid." He continued on, and the metal clanked heavily into place. "Smooth as silk." He grinned widely, glancing over at Lex and Violet. "Your turn."

Lex climbed over the top of the turnstile with ease, axe in one hand, and threw Joe a smug expression when she reached the other side without making a sound.

He rolled his eyes. "Stop trying to impress me. You know you're not my type."

Her frosty scowl was all Joe needed to stop talking. Violet attempted to replicate Lex's method for passing over the turnstiles but lost her balance when climbing and dropped her crowbar with a clatter. She clenched her jaw as the sound rang out painfully.

"Sorry."

Joe grinned, picking up the weapon and helping her over. "Don't worry."

Violet was fairly sure she heard Lex mutter something

about 'idiots' but did her best to blow past it. They headed on, footsteps muffled by the dusty floor. There were no windows as they got further into the building, so Joe reached into his backpack for their flashlights. Violet clicked hers on, and after a few flickers, a thin beam of yellow light illuminated her path. She needed new batteries—these weren't going to last much longer.

The double doors up ahead led to the communal changing rooms. Lex put her hand out to open them, but Joe stopped her. "Wait." There was an odd smile on his face.

"What?"

"Nothing, just... I've never really thought about it before."

"Thought about what?" Lex sounded impatient.

"Naked zombies."

She raised an eyebrow. "Why *would* you think about that?"

"We're about to go into the changing rooms. What if someone got bitten while they were getting dressed?"

Violet shook her head dismissively. "You don't turn right away; they'd have time to put some pants on at least."

Joe thought for a moment. "I bet we see a naked zombie."

Lex's eyes glittered. "I'll take that bet." If there was one thing she liked as much as blood and destruction, it was any form of gambling or competition.

"What have you got?" Joe asked.

"A pack of potato chips."

"Unopened?"

"Of course, who do you think I am?"

"What do you want for them?"

"I want you to shave that thing off your face."

Joe's eyes widened. "Not the 'stache?"

"Yes."

"But... it's glorious."

"No, it's thin and gross and makes you look like a creepy stalker."

Joe turned to Violet for support, but she bit her lip. "I think that's a good deal, Joe."

He narrowed his brow. "*You* hate the 'stache, too?"

"I didn't say that."

"She does hate it," Lex piped up helpfully. "Because she has eyes."

Joe held up his hands. "Fine. If you win, I'll shave Maurice."

"Maurice?"

"That's what I named it."

Lex and Violet threw each other sideways glances but said nothing, heading into the changing rooms silently.

There was a terrible smell, and it didn't take long to discover the source. The huge room was divided into cubicles, and many of these had been converted into small bedrooms for the people who used to live here. They were now home to rotting corpses. Violet didn't know much about the illness that had killed this community, only that it clearly included a lot of vomiting and blood. The bodies were shriveled, bloodied, and barely recognizable as human. She averted her gaze as they passed a couple, arms around each other, rotting into the floor beneath them.

"What a horrible way to go," she murmured.

Lex shrugged. "Eaten by zombies is probably worse."

The changing rooms had apparently been lived in for a long time. There were blankets and pillows in each cubicle, children's chalk drawings on the walls, toys and games scattered across the floor. There were a lot of corpses, each with dried blood around their noses and eyes and congealed vomit on their clothes. It appeared that the children had been the first to go, as most of these had been taken to the largest cubicle and covered with sheets. Violet assumed there had been plans to bury or burn them, but the illness ensured there had not been enough time. The adults seemed to have died in their rooms or just fallen as they walked. As yet, there were no signs of survivors or biters.

"Okay, I think I'm ready," Joe said confidently.

"Ready for what?" Violet asked, tearing her eyes away from the body of a man hanging from a short noose. Clearly, he had not wanted to wait for the sickness to claim him. She wondered why no one had taken him down. Was he the last to go?

"Joe thinks he can make me laugh," Lex answered, already sounding bored.

Violet was confused. "You laugh at Joe all the time."

"*At* him. Because he's an idiot. Not because he's funny."

"That's going to change," Joe insisted, "because I've got some absolute crackers about swimming pools." He cleared his throat dramatically. "Where do zombies like to go swimming?"

"I don't know," Lex replied.

"The Dead Sea!"

Violet stopped walking, giving Joe her most scathing look. Lex didn't even crack a smile.

He shrugged. "They can't all be winners."

Unfortunately for the two women, Joe continued to treat them to a barrage of swimming pool comedy as they explored. Violet hadn't thought it possible, but the first one had actually been the best.

"Okay, okay, this is the one," Joe began. "This'll be the one that gets you laughing."

"That would be a nice change," Violet said, and Lex grinned.

"Why should you never swim on a full stomach?"

"Why?"

"Because it's easier to swim in water."

"No, Joe. That's not the one."

He thought for a moment. "What stroke do sheep like best? The baaaaaackstroke."

"Please stop."

"I've got more, don't worry. How do you drown a blonde?"

"Tell her these jokes?" Lex suggested. "Because I may not be blonde, but I want to drown myself right now."

"You put a scratch and sniff sticker at the bottom of the pool."

"Joe, shut up," Violet said.

"I could do this all ni—"

"No, I mean shut up. Listen." Violet stopped walking, craning her head. She was sure she'd heard something just a moment ago. Joe was listening now, too. Lex gripped her axe tightly.

Splashing. Something was moving in the pool up ahead. They headed to the end of the room, where natural light poured through a large archway.

They were inside the huge room with the pool. On the wall to the right were large windows, dirty and with a couple of cracks, but intact. In front of the windows was a tall waterslide, accessible by a long, spiralling set of steps. The slide let out in a separate pool, surrounded by a low glass wall and only accessible via a metal ladder in the water. Over to the left of the room was a small wooden structure, which Violet supposed was a sauna. The main pool held three biters, bobbing around in the middle of the dark green water.

"Anyone fancy a dip?" Joe asked, lowering his crowbar. He moved closer to the pool.

"Careful," Violet said, eyes on the zombies.

"Don't worry, they can't get out."

He was right—the biters seemed able to keep their heads above the water most of the time but unable to co-ordinate anything like swimming. They were bloated, as though they'd been in there for weeks, with features so distorted that their faces appeared more like stretched rubber Halloween masks than people.

"Do you think there are more at the bottom?" Joe asked. "Once they get too waterlogged, I can't imagine there'd be much keeping them up."

Violet shuddered at the thought.

"Should we take them out?" Lex asked.

Why would we want to take them out? They're trapped in there.

Oh, she means 'Take them out'.

"No, just leave them," Joe said. He glanced around the huge room. "I think the rest of this place is secure." He jerked his head at the little wooden structure. "What's that?"

Lex followed his gaze. "The sauna."

Joe moved over to investigate. Lex splashed the water with her axe, causing the zombies to become more excited. They bobbed up and down as they attempted to reach her.

"I hate not being able to kill them," she groaned.

"Yeah, me too," Violet lied. In reality, she was more than happy to leave them out of reach. It lowered her chances of tripping over her own feet and falling face-first into them.

"Yes!" Joe stood triumphantly at the other side of the room, pointing at the open door behind him.

"What is it?" Violet called.

"A naked zombie!" Joe looked so thrilled, holding his now-bloodied crowbar in the air. "I knew we'd find one! Come here."

"No thanks," Violet replied, but Lex was already marching over. "You're going to see?"

"Yeah, he could be lying."

Less tempted by the thought of a corpse with no clothes on, Violet decided to stay put. It was also surprisingly difficult to draw herself away from the biters in the water. The creatures were usually intrinsically terrifying, with the power to kill and infect anyone in their reach, but these three were just splashing around like kittens in a pond.

She glanced over as Lex swore loudly from the other side of the room. Joe was celebrating her discovery of the naked biter with what Violet assumed was a kind of dance. It certainly involved a lot of high kicks and spinning, though she thought it could've done without the continual thrusting. But suddenly, his smile faded.

"Violet, run!"

She spun around just in time. Three zombies were charging from the changing room and heading straight for her—two women in lifeguard attire and a man in a yellow Speedo. One of the lifeguards ran to the sauna, but the two remaining biters headed straight for Violet. She turned, charging the other way around the pool. Lex cried out excitedly, and Violet caught a glimpse of her burying the axe in the lifeguard's head. Joe was running over from the other direction, holding up his crowbar.

"Duck!" he yelled when he reached her, and Violet did. Joe smashed the crowbar into the other lifeguard. Violet turned, raising her own, but the biter in the Speedo was too quick. As they collided, he knocked the weapon from her grasp. It clattered heavily onto the floor a few feet away before sliding into the water. She fought to hold the zombie back. Nearby, Joe was bashing in the head of the lifeguard, but there were now two more zombies approaching. Lex was still at the other side of the pool, burying her axe into the brain of a third. The one grappling with Violet snapped his teeth just inches from her face.

I cannot be killed by a zombie dressed in a Speedo.

Calm down. He's not killed you yet.

Violet forced the zombie back a few feet, but without a weapon and with Joe fighting off two more biters on his own, she was helpless.

You can do this. You've been fighting these things for the past year. You're tough, you're stronger than you—

But as the two of them struggled, Violet lost her footing and fell into the water, realizing she was not, in fact, stronger than she thought.

FOUR

VIOLET PLUNGED INTO THE COLD, GREEN WATER. HER clothes became heavy, and she worked hard to swim back up to the surface, managing to get a lungful of oxygen before the Speedo zombie fell on top of her. His weight forced them both under. She could see nothing through the stinging, vile water. The biter was trying to grab hold of her arms, but she managed to break free of his grasp. She made for the surface again, able to pull forward a few feet before Speedo grabbed hold of her leg and forced her back down. Her chest began to pound as her lungs cried out for air. She tried to shake the creature off, but he was holding on too tightly, his nails breaking through the skin on her leg. Her lungs felt as though they were about to burst.

There was a sound, and another set of hands grabbed Violet's shoulders and pulled her back. She kicked her legs vigorously, and the biter was finally dislodged. The hands on her shoulders pulled her back to the surface. Breaking through the slimy surface, she gasped for air, choking out the disgusting green sludge, then turned to see what had grabbed her. Joe was treading water at her side and gave a quick smile.

"Alright?"

His eyes scanned the space below. Seconds later, Speedo popped up through the water, bobbing around clumsily just a few feet away. Violet didn't have her weapon anymore, and it seemed that neither did Joe. The biter let out a hiss, splashing violently in its attempts to close the gap between them. But suddenly it stopped paddling and fell forward in the water, floating face down. Violet saw a knife lodged in the back of its skull and looked up. Lex stood at the edge of the pool, grinning triumphantly.

"Did you throw that?" Violet asked. Lex gave a little bow.

"How did you know it would hit him?" Joe asked.

"I didn't, I was aiming for that thing on your face."

"Not Maurice?"

"Stop calling it that."

There were more dead bodies surrounding the pool, their dark blood beginning to run down into the water. "Did you kill all of those?" Violet asked.

"I did a few," Joe piped up.

"He killed two, I handled the rest," Lex corrected. "I'd get out now if I were you, unless you're planning on some synchronized swimming with those guys."

Violet turned and saw the three water-biters slowly approaching.

"Come on," Joe said paddling to the edge of the pool.

"WHAT HAPPENED TO YOU?" JACK ASKED WHEN VIOLET and Joe dropped onto one of the couches in the café. The two of them were dripping wet, tinted green, and stank of stagnant water. Violet examined the cuts on her legs where the biter had grabbed her. They weren't deep. As long as she could avoid infection from the rancid water, she'd be okay.

"We went for a swim," she answered simply.

"Why?"

Joe's voice was flat. "It wasn't a choice we made."

Realization settled on Jack's face. "Oh, right."

"The pool is clear," Lex said, cleaning the blood off her axe. "Shall we get started?"

Jack pointed to the corner. "There are some empty boxes over there. We can start by filling those with any food you can find."

"Ow!"

Ryan, standing a few feet away, dropped his bachete, cradling his hand. Violet smelled the blood before she saw it. He'd cut himself on his weapon. The blood—so sweet smelling, so delicious—was already making her feel dizzy. Joe, who was less experienced in this than she was, gripped the sides of his chair. There wasn't much time. She got to her feet, "Joe, we need to go and do that thing."

"What thing?" he asked, watching hypnotically as Ella hurried over to patch Ryan up.

"The *thing*," Violet insisted pointedly, grabbing his arm.

"Oh yeah," he muttered, stumbling as he got to his feet. "Yeah, that thing. Let's do that now." He began to move to the door, but Violet knew his legs, like her own, were as heavy as lead. Somehow, they managed to get clear of the café. Joe was struggling even more than she was, and kept darting glances over his shoulder. She loosened her grip on his arm and took his hand, pulling him firmly and stepping through the first door she found. It was the women's bathroom. She pushed Joe over to the sinks.

"Splash your face," she ordered. "It helps."

He nodded, slowly reaching for the tap, but the water was off. He groaned, turning and moving to the wall. Violet went into the nearest stall and opened the top of the system. There was still water inside. She reached down, cupping the liquid in her hands. "Here."

Joe raised an eyebrow. "No thanks, I'm good."

"You need to put this on your face."

"It's *toilet water*."

Her voice was firm. "Joe, your pupils are dilated, you're sweating, and you can barely stand up. If you turn, I don't know if I can keep you hidden. So get over here and splash the disgusting water on your face."

Joe scowled but did as he was told. Afterward, he slid down onto the floor.

"Are you okay?" Violet asked.

"I was. Before the toilet water." But he was smiling.

That had been too close. Just because Joe had eaten yesterday didn't mean he wouldn't feed again today. The monster inside each of them was never sated, it always wanted more.

But Joe was beginning to look a little better. "Do you think you're ready to go back?" she asked.

He nodded, holding out his hand and allowing her to pull him to his feet.

"Does it get easier?" he asked. "You seemed to handle it pretty well."

"It gets easier to control, but the hunger is the same. I still wanted to rip Ryan's hand off."

"That's comforting."

She shrugged. "Hey, it's still better than being dead, right?"

"So's a massive heart attack, but I'm not begging for one of those, either."

When they returned to the café, Ryan was patched up and once again trying to impress Ella with his bachete skills, tossing the weapon into the air and catching it with his good hand.

Joe caught Violet's eye. "Why do I feel like I'll be splashing toilet water on my face again soon?" he muttered.

Jack glanced up from behind the counter, where he was dropping things into a bag. "Everything okay?"

Violet smiled in what she hoped was a sincere way. "Yeah, we just had to..." She realized she had no reasonable explanation as to why she and Joe had needed to leave the room together so urgently. Luckily, Joe swooped in to save the day.

"Violet had to show me something."

Jack raised an eyebrow. "Show you something?"

Violet wasn't altogether sure where Joe was going with this, but she decided to ride it out. Clearly, he had some kind of plan.

Joe nodded casually. "Yeah. It was a medical thing. She wanted my opinion."

Violet's eyes widened, mortified. That was *not* what

she'd had in mind. Unfortunately, she had no choice but to go along with it. "Yeah. I just... I thought Joe would know what it was."

Great, now Jack's imagining what the hideous it is. Just stop talking.

Jack seemed to physically recoil. "Oh. Okay." He turned away, moving over to a small room at the back of the café.

"You're welcome," Joe mouthed.

Violet decided to spend the rest of the day planning how, exactly, she would kill him.

THEY PACKED UP ALL THE FOOD THEY COULD FIND AND arranged to come back the following day for a final sweep. There was no sign of any medicine, but Ezra's source had assured him it was there. Violet had no idea who Ezra's mysterious 'source' was, and she couldn't help but feel mildly irritated that this person didn't come to the gross pool with the diseased corpses themselves, but that wasn't how things worked in Harmony. Ezra would get tips from his sources, which would be relayed to one of the scavenging groups, and then it was their job to follow it up.

As they headed out to the vehicles, Violet spotted movement from the other side of the parking lot.

"Stop," she hissed, pointing for the others to see. They followed her gaze.

"Is it biters?" Lex asked, squinting.

"It's lions," Joe answered matter-of-factly. Violet could see them clearly now—there were three lions over by the fence. A male and two females.

"Uh... why are there lions in the parking lot?" Ryan asked, clutching the bachete tightly.

"Must've escaped from the zoo," Jack suggested. "There's one not too far from here."

"Or someone let them out," Ella added.

Lex raised an eyebrow. "Why would anyone do that?"

"I guess they didn't want them to starve to death," muttered Violet. The lions had spotted their group and were currently observing them curiously.

"Well isn't that thoughtful?" Joe said. "I would hate for the lions to go hungry. I wonder what they've been eating?" His tone suggested he had more than one idea about what the animals might've been living on.

Jack started walking back to the vehicles. "Let's get out of here before more turn up."

"More?" Violet didn't like the sound of that.

"If they're from the zoo a couple of towns over, then there are at least twelve."

"Yeah, let's go." Violet hurried to the truck with the others. It would be just her luck to survive the zompocalypse only to be eaten by a big cat.

THAT EVENING, WHEN VIOLET STARTLED BACK TO CONsciousness from another nightmare, she managed to silence her sobs before Joe woke up. Rocking back and forth slowly on her bed, she tried to calm herself by running her fingers over the raised flesh of her scar, but she couldn't get her heart to stop racing. The room felt suffocating. She had to get out. She needed air.

Slowly, doing all she could not to wake Joe, she got out of bed and left the room, not caring that she was barefoot and in her pajamas. She slipped out of the apartment, down the stairs, and out into the cold air. It made her feel better, but it wasn't enough. Her mind was still racing, images of things she didn't want to remember flinging themselves to the forefront. She ran, trying to put as much distance as she could between herself and the memories, but it was no use. After fighting for so long to keep them at bay, she could no longer hold them back, and they began to flood through the barriers she'd so carefully constructed.

MATT GLANCED UP WHEN VIOLET CAME INTO THE ROOM.

He smiled. *"You look beautiful."*

"Thanks," answered Joe casually, as he entered behind her and moved toward the fruit bowl.

"Clearly I was talking to Violet."

Joe shrugged, taking a bite out of an apple. *"I took a chance."*

Violet grinned, trying to ignore the flush in her cheeks. She didn't think she looked beautiful in the same ripped jeans she'd worn for weeks and a shirt that was probably three sizes too big. Her hair was a mess, and she could do with a little more sleep, but Matt never noticed those things. The two of them were still dancing around it, but when Joe got bitten a month ago and thought he was going to die, he had decided to 'helpfully' tell Violet that Matt had feelings for her. She supposed she should've picked up on it before. It wasn't like he made it obvious, but there was an occasional lingering glance, times when it'd seemed like he wanted to tell her something but then backed out at the last moment. Unfortunately, Violet didn't have much experience with flirting or relationships, and she'd always breezed past these moments without a second thought.

Now that she knew how he felt, she supposed she should really try to untangle what her own feelings were for him. That was the hard part, because if she were honest, she had no idea. Guys had never exactly fallen over themselves to date her. In fact, she could count on one hand the number of dates she'd been on.

Actually, she could count on two fingers the number of dates she'd been on.

She knew she cared for Matt. A lot. Did she love him? Probably, but she loved Joe, too, and Toby. Having survived so much of the zompocalypse together, it was hard to stay casual. The question was, did she love Matt in the same way she loved the other two, or was it something more? She still wasn't sure about that part. Ever since fleeing the lab where they'd been held prisoner, they'd spent weeks running from the dead, searching for a safe place, and hunting down supplies. During that time, Toby had gotten really sick, and they'd been so worried about keeping him alive that all thoughts of 'does he like-me like-me?'

went out the window.

But now they were safe, maybe she could actually pause and think about the Matt situation. They had the time, at least. She just needed to get today over with.

She sat down at the table opposite Matt. In the weeks since they'd arrived at the cottage, he'd barely changed at all. His eyes were the same green, his messy hair the same dark brown, though it had been recently hacked at slightly by Violet because she'd thought 'How hard could it be to give it a trim?' Turned out, the answer was—incredibly. But Matt, ever the gentleman, had told her she'd done great. It would've been more convincing if Joe and Toby hadn't been laughing raucously throughout, but the thought was there.

"Are you sure about this?" Violet asked, the familiar anxious feeling rising in the pit of her stomach.

Matt nodded. "If we want enough supplies so that we don't need to go out again for a while, we have to hit somewhere big." He gestured to the map on the table. "This warehouse should be full of enough cans to last us for months, maybe longer. We just take the truck and load up as much as we can get."

"But what if—"

Matt cut her off. "Joe and I checked it out a few days ago. We couldn't see any signs of biters. If that's changed, we'll give the place up and try somewhere else."

But it wasn't the biters that had been their biggest problem. It was people. When Violet and her friends arrived at the warehouse, there was a car outside.

"This wasn't here last time, was it?" Joe asked.

"I can't remember," Matt replied. "I don't think so."

"What shall we do?"

Matt looked up at the huge grey building. "Let's keep going."

When they stepped into the warehouse, they saw the others straight away—two men and two women, talking quietly just inside the doors. They turned, eyes wide, when they saw Violet and the guys. One of the men raised a pistol.

"Whoa, relax," Joe said, holding up his hands. "We're

here for supplies, just like you."

"Find somewhere else," the man with the gun growled, lowering it barely an inch.

"There's enough here for all of us." Matt's voice was gentle, unthreatening. He had a way of speaking that was almost always able to diffuse people's anger. One of the women held out her hand and pushed the gun down.

"He's right, Neil. We're not going to start killing the living for some cans of tuna."

The man paused, then tucked his gun into the back of his pants.

"Let's split into two groups," the woman suggested, her blue eyes focused on Matt. "You and the kid are with Neil and I."

Matt didn't sound happy about this. "Why don't we stick with our own people?"

"Because I don't trust you." Her voice was cold. "You stay with me, or you can find somewhere else. It's your choice."

Violet didn't like the idea of splitting up, but she could already see the warehouse was full to bursting with food. They couldn't afford to turn down such a great opportunity.

"What do you think?" Matt asked, while the woman gave instructions to her group in a low voice.

"I think this is our best bet for supplies," Violet admitted.

"You're happy to split up?"

"If that's how she says it has to go."

Matt agreed, so he, Toby, and Ben headed off. The sinking feeling in Violet's stomach had turned to quicksand. Was this a bad idea? It was too late to change her mind. She watched Matt, Toby, and the dog disappear down one of the long rows of shelves and tried to tell herself that her sense of helplessness was nothing more than nerves.

She didn't know exactly what happened after that. Toby hadn't been able to remember much when he eventually started talking again. He, Matt, Neil, and the woman—who still hadn't given her name—had walked along several of the huge shelving units, gathering supplies as they went. As they rounded one corner, they'd found themselves facing at least thirty zombies. Several of the creatures had seen them immediately, and their cries had alerted the others. In the confusion, Neil fired his gun and Matt had been shot in the leg.

They'd fled, heading back to Violet and the others. She'd seen Ben first, barking as he ran, and then the two strangers. Toby and Matt had been at the back, Toby trying desperately to hold Matt up as he ran. He let go of him for a moment, pulling one of the shelving units down to buy some time, but there were too many biters. Already they were climbing over the debris, screaming hungrily as they continued their chase. Toby rejoined Matt, who was still relatively fast despite his leg bleeding heavily, which Violet smelled before she could see.

She didn't know what to do. If she got any closer and tried to help, she'd lose control and rip him apart. Joe would do the same, and so they had no choice but to watch helplessly as the biters got nearer and nearer to their friends. Violet was screaming their names, yelling at them to run. Joe was begging the strangers to go and help, but they were already fleeing the warehouse.

Matt glanced behind him, then dislodged his arm from Toby's shoulder. He was shouting now, telling him to go. Toby tried to take hold of his arm again, but Matt pushed him roughly away.

"Go," he yelled, his eyes on Violet now. "Run!"

"No!" Violet screamed. But the biters were so close. Joe was crying out for Matt to move. Toby made one last attempt to force him forward, but it didn't work. The boy had no choice, and with a final desperate glance at Violet and Joe, broke into a sprint. Joe grabbed him, pushing him in the direction of the door. Matt and Violet had a moment, just one, before the biters broke over him like a wave. In that second, their eyes met, and he gave her a small smile. A smile that seemed to say, 'Don't worry, you'll be okay.'

Then he was gone, overcome by the horde which dragged him out of view. She screamed again, but now there were hands on her arms. Joe and Toby were pulling her, kicking and screaming, from the warehouse.

BLOODY TEARS STREAMED DOWN HER FACE. SHE HADN'T realized she was crying, and she wiped her cheeks roughly. It had been her fault. If she hadn't agreed to split up, if she'd just said they needed to leave the warehouse and go somewhere else, Matt would still be alive.

His death haunted her every moment, even when she wasn't specifically thinking about it. She knew she should be grateful to still have Joe and Toby. She had new friends and a safe place to live. But it didn't matter. Her old friends only reminded her of the one she had lost. The new ones were nice, but they didn't compare to Matt, to what he'd meant to her. They couldn't understand her obscure movie references or make her laugh with just a sideways look. She'd have chosen being scared with Matt over being safe in Harmony any day.

"Violet?"

Jack approached, eyes darting around cautiously. It was against the rules to be outside after dark. Ezra said it was for their protection—that way, the soldiers knew any movement inside the community was either intruders or biters. Getting caught out here could cost Violet a week's worth of points, but luckily, it was Jack who'd found her, and they were practically friends.

"What are you doing?" he asked, crouching at her side. He turned her face gently to see more clearly in the moonlight. "What happened?"

Oh, that's right. The eye blood.

"I had a nose bleed."

"It's all over your face."

Violet was too tired to think of an explanation. "Why are you here?"

"I'm on duty. You're lucky I recognized you. You could've been shot. Come on." He got to his feet, helping her up. "Let's get you home."

"WELL, THIS IS A GOOD START."

Violet had to agree with Joe's assessment. They were parked outside the pool building in the truck with Jack. Parked by the entrance was a school bus, the sides of which were streaked with bloody handprints. Its door was open, and a woman's legs stuck out.

"Do you think anyone made it?" Violet asked.

"Maybe," Jack replied.

"Do you think they went inside?"

"I'd say so."

"So, we should go the other way, right?" Joe leaned back in his seat. "We don't know what these people are like."

"He's got a point, they could be dangerous," Violet said, nodding.

They could also be bleeding, and I don't feel like eating anyone today.

But Jack shook his head. "They might need our help. You know what Ezra said about survivors—the more people we have inside our walls, the fewer biters we have outside."

Before Violet had a chance to argue, he was already out of the truck and heading to the front doors, where Lex and the others were waiting.

She sighed. "I guess we should—"

47

"We absolutely shouldn't," Joe interrupted. "This is clearly a terrible idea."

"Yep," she agreed, opening the door and getting out, holding onto her new crowbar tightly. After losing her old one, this replacement had cost ten points.

One of the glass front doors had a bloodied handprint smeared across it, just like the sides of the bus. Joe regarded the door with zero enthusiasm as he hoisted his backpack onto his shoulders. "This looks hopeful."

"We'll stick together," Jack said. "Search for survivors first."

"What if they're dangerous?" Ella asked, biting her lip.

"*We're* dangerous," Lex said. "They should be scared of *us*." She reached for the door and swung it open, stepping inside without the slightest hint of fear. Jack grinned and followed her.

Ryan groaned. "This is a really bad idea," he said, but he went in, too, closely followed, as always, by Ella.

Joe turned to Violet. "Just remember—if they're dangerous and we get caught, I'm deaf and you don't speak English."

"That's foolproof."

Joe winked, and together they headed into the building. It seemed darker inside than yesterday. The doors swung shut heavily behind them, and Violet thought the sound had a finality to it she hadn't heard the day before. The air was thick, as though the dust coating everything had recently been stirred up. Jack shone his flashlight around, and the beam of light settled on the path to the café. Footsteps in the dust led to and from that direction.

"Are those ours from yesterday?" Ella asked.

"Probably," Jack replied, "but they could also belong to whoever drove the bus. Let's check it out."

Each member of the group carried their weapon with intent. Joe had chosen to bring a baseball bat. Ella and Lex both had axes, whereas Jack was trying out a crossbow he'd found a few days ago and had been practicing with inside the walls. Ryan still had his bachete, and Violet just hoped he didn't accidentally cut his arm off, which, if yesterday was anything to go by, was a tall order for him.

Jack led them to the café, which was clear of survivors and biters. Violet supposed she should have felt reassured by this, but she couldn't fight the feeling that something horrible was about to happen.

"Come on," Jack ordered, heading back the way they came and leading them on toward the pool. His tone was brisk. It was clear he thought they were in danger and wanted to get in and out as quickly as possible. They walked in silence, flashlights panning the hallway for any signs of movement. Violet's light died within moments, the batteries finally giving up, so she stuck close to Joe.

No more than a minute later, a familiar smell pricked at her nostrils. Joe slowed his pace, catching the scent, too.

"Blood," Lex said. Droplets of blood, some small, some the size of a hand, had soaked into the dust on the floor.

"It's fresh," Violet said, catching Joe's eye.

"How do you know?" Ella asked.

She shrugged. "It just looks fresh." It wasn't like she could tell the truth—that she could smell the difference between old blood and that which had been spilled within the last few minutes.

"It's definitely new," Lex confirmed. "It wasn't here yesterday. We would've seen it. Besides, we know there are people here, and all the signs so far hardly suggest they're having a great day."

The others continued on, but Violet paused, eyes still on the stain. There wasn't too much, and it had dried enough to allow her to maintain control of herself, but the fact that it was fresh meant there was probably someone actively bleeding close by.

"What do you think happened?" Joe asked, hanging back.

"The same thing that always happens," she sighed, moving on to catch up with the others outside the doors to the changing rooms. Another bloody handprint was streaked across the wood surface of the doors.

"I'm sensing a theme here," muttered Ella.

"Ah, a bloody handprint. That's practically a Welcome sign these days."

Matt's voice popped into Violet's head out of nowhere.

She couldn't remember when he'd said that, but it sounded so clear that it was all she could do not to turn around and check he wasn't right behind her. She shook the memory away. She didn't need to be thinking about him right now.

"Let's just get this over with," Jack said, moving inside.

The rest of the group followed. Violet tried to remain hopeful. There was still the possibility, however slim, that there were no biters. Perhaps whoever had left the blood trail and handprint had managed to give their undead pursuers the slip?

Her optimism was shattered, however, the moment she stepped into the changing rooms and found a fresh corpse. It was a man, not long dead. He had been half eaten. What was left of his insides were ripped out and scattered all around him. The blood was thick, but thankfully the blood of corpses didn't affect Violet or Joe, regardless of how recently the person had died. Considering the number of dead bodies they stumbled upon on a regular basis, that was a useful distinction.

Ryan knelt, taking a knife out of his pocket and gently sliding it into the skull of the man, ensuring he didn't get back up again.

Continuing through the changing rooms, they found no signs of survivors, but several more corpses littered their path. Some had been biters, as evidenced by the missing heads or stab wounds in their skulls. Most of the bodies, though, were living people who'd only recently been killed and at least partially eaten. This was often the case for those who were attacked by biters—the creatures would feed on their bodies until something new and fresh came along. It was rare they'd strip a corpse to the bone, which was why so many people who'd been half-chewed up came back as zombies themselves.

"I guess they put up a hell of a fight," Jack mused, turning over one of the biters with his foot. It had a screwdriver lodged in its eye socket.

Ryan shrugged. "Didn't do them much good. They're still dead."

"I had just been thinking this morning that this place

didn't feel as hopeless and depressing as I'd like," Joe sighed.

Lex rolled her eyes, swinging her axe casually as she walked. "You know, the zombies are less annoying than you."

Joe looked as though he were about to say something, but he was interrupted by the sound of screaming. They all froze.

"Come on," Jack ordered, breaking into a run and heading toward the pool. Violet and the others were close behind.

They found chaos. There were at least twelve more biters in the green water, splashing and bobbing around clumsily. There were some other bodies, too, all floating face down. More corpses littered the floor around the pool—the group from the bus must've been big. At the other end of the room were ten biters, all desperately trying to get into the sauna. Their pale, filthy hands pummeled against the door and walls.

"Do you think there are people in there?" Joe whispered to Violet.

She nodded. "Why else would they be trying to get inside?"

"We should go," Ella hissed. "We can't take on that many, not without help. We should go home and get more soldiers."

Jack shook his head. "By the time we leave and come back..."

He didn't need to finish. Violet knew what he was saying. The people weren't going to last much longer, not with the biters fighting so hard to get in. She caught sight of a little girl, no more than five years old, behind the glass door as one of the biters shifted to the side. Violet's heart caught in her throat.

"We have to help them," she insisted.

"We should split up," Jack muttered. "Approach the biters on each side. They'll have to split up to reach all of us, and it'll be easier to handle them in smaller groups."

"That's still five biters to three of us," Joe said. "We'll be outnumbered, and that's with an even split. We can't be sure that will happen."

"Trust me." Jack's voice was controlled. "We can handle it. We've done it before."

"I've done lots of things before that I never want to do again. Cosplay, for instance."

"Let's just do it," Lex interrupted, heading to the left. Ryan and Jack followed. Violet, Joe, and Ella turned to the right. Their journey was longer, as they needed to make their way around the length of the pool, past the spiral staircase to the water slide, and on toward the sauna. So far, the dead had been too distracted by the survivors inside the small structure to notice the group outside. Violet wasn't sure how long that would last.

When both groups were in position, Jack gave Joe a hand signal, and the pair of them started yelling to get the zombies attention. Three turned to Jack's group, seven to Joe's.

Oh, come on!

"This is not an even split," Joe yelled, as he, Violet, and Ella began backing up. Violet held up her crowbar, but she knew she'd never stand a chance against this many. The zombies screamed as they ran for the three of them at full speed.

"Run!" Jack called over, firing his crossbow at the biter closest to Violet. The arrow went straight through its eye. Lex buried her axe into the face of the zombie that was about to grab Jack while he reloaded.

"Come on, Violet!" Joe pulled her arm, forcing her to run with him. Ella was close behind. Violet's chest pounded. Six biters against her, Joe, and Ella. Without guns, there was no way they'd make it. Even if she could survive infection, she wasn't immune to being torn apart.

Just keep running. Get around to Jack and the others, and then we have more of a chance.

A scream. Not a biter this time. Violet turned just in time to see Ella slip and fall into the pool.

"No!" She made to go back, but two of the pursuing zombies jumped into the water after Ella, forcing her under. Joe pulled at Violet's hand, but she was frozen, watching as dark, red blood bubbled to the surface.

"Move," Joe ordered, yanking Violet roughly.

She began to run again but quickly lost her balance on the slick surface, slipping and stumbling precariously, falling onto her knees. Somehow, she was able to avoid tumbling into the pool just an inch from her fingertips, but she lost her grip on the crowbar. It slid along the floor and into the murky water, sinking immediately.

Sonofa—

"Leave it," Joe grunted, helping Violet to her feet.

"It cost me ten points!"

"You want to go back for it?"

She groaned, breaking into a run. Joe kept close to her side, and they headed back in the direction of the changing rooms. Jack and the others appeared to have the same idea. They had killed all of their biters. All that were left were the four still chasing Violet and Joe. Less than one apiece. They could handle that as a group.

But as Violet knew by now, life was never easy, and more biters suddenly appeared in the archway to the changing rooms, cutting off their exit. They were moving too fast to count, but there were a lot. Most charged toward Jack and the others, but several had noticed Violet and Joe and ran in their direction, too.

"Up here." Joe took her hand again, leading her toward the water slide's spiral staircase.

"Are you serious?"

"I have to ride it at least once." He let her climb the stairs first. She held onto the blue railing with sweaty hands as she stumbled up the steep spiral. The slide was high, and the steps seemed endless.

"Joe?" she called out, not turning back. Violet knew well enough that if she turned, she'd fall flat on her face.

"I'm here, keep going."

She could hear more than just their two pairs of feet on the steps now. Joe made a noise, and the railing shook. Violet's stomach dropped. Had he lost his footing? Had they gotten him? She glanced over her shoulder, but he was still behind her. Whatever had been chasing them, he'd kicked it back down.

"Keep going," he repeated, pushing her on.

They reached the top. She looked at Joe expectantly. He leaned over the side, eyes focused on the spiral steps, and swore. The biters were making their way back up again.

"What do we do?" she asked.

He thought for a moment, then nodded to the dark tube to their left. "What comes up..."

Of course.

They got onto their hands and knees, then crawled through the entrance to the blue tunnel, Joe's baseball bat clunking along the hard surface as he moved. The tube itself wasn't very steep, and without the water to push them along, it seemed to take an eternity to travel through. It was enclosed for the first part, but after a while, opened out. Violet stopped, leaning over the side to see what was happening down below. There had to be at least twenty biters around the pool now. The people from the sauna had gotten out and were fighting, but there were only six or seven of them. Jack and Lex were fighting side by side, him firing shots with the crossbow, her slicing off the heads of any ghouls that got too close. Ryan was standing on top of a plant pot, swinging his bachete enthusiastically. The lack of corpses around him suggested he'd done little to help the cause so far. The small girl had vanished.

Joe exhaled. "This is crazy."

"What should we do?"

"If we can get down to the bottom we can climb out of the little pool and go help." He paused. "Or, you know, run away. I'm happy with either." There was a noise behind him, hands slapping against the smooth floor of the slide.

They followed us.

VIOLET HAD HOPED THAT ONCE THE BITERS GOT TO the top of the steps and found nothing, they'd either go back down or at least just stand around for a while rather than immediately crawling into the tunnel. She was learning that being hopeful about anything to do with biters was more than a little naïve.

She crawled on, into the next enclosed segment. They continued in darkness, the sounds of the biters fading a little but not disappearing. They were still coming.

"These things are a lot less fun without the water," Joe puffed.

Soon, they reached the bottom. The pool beneath the end of the tube was green and stagnant. She couldn't see the floor.

Anything could be under there.

What's your other choice? Stay in here?

The sound of movement not far behind demonstrated that this wasn't an option. As quickly as she could, Violet lowered herself into the water, and began wading to the ladder on the other side. Joe splashed down too, following her to the only way out. As yet, nothing had grabbed her legs or attempted to pull her under. Successfully reaching the ladder, she struggled to climb out of the water. It was hard—her wet clothes weighed her down.

S
I
X

"Little faster, Vi," Joe began, as the biters from the slide dropped into the pool. It was shallow enough for them to keep their feet on the ground, and they splashed clumsily toward the pair.

Violet gripped the metal bars tightly, pulling herself out. The zombies were closing the gap, but she took Joe's hand and helped wrench him out of the water just as they reached the ladder. Joe and Violet watched the zombies fumble clumsily, clearly lacking the coordination to be able to climb. They were contained, for now, screaming and hissing hungrily as they clawed at the edge of the pool.

Violet's eyes swept the room. To the right there was a clear path to the changing rooms. They could also keep going in that direction to reach their friends. Jack and Lex were still fighting, and Ryan seemed to actually be helping now, downing one biter that approached Lex from behind. Violet could only see two other survivors, but there were at least eight biters still active, and though she wanted nothing more than to get out of this place, Violet couldn't leave her friends to fight them alone. She just needed to find a weapon.

There had to be something on the floor near Jack, a weapon one of the fallen survivors had dropped. But as she and Joe began to head over, more biters appeared at the entrance to the changing rooms. A couple headed for Jack and the others, but the rest of the zombies charged full speed for the two of them.

Joe grabbed her arm. "There's another way out over here, come on."

They hurried through a door to their left, slamming it shut behind them. The room was dark, but while Joe held the door closed Violet found the lock and slid it into place. The biters pounded on the other side.

Joe stepped back, leaning his hands on his knees and panting a little. "This place really sucks."

Violet had to agree. She glanced around, taking in their surroundings. They were in a storeroom filled with pool equipment and toys, with another door on the other side of the room.

"We should check that out," she said. "We might be able to get back around to the others."

"Or we could get the hell out of here," Joe countered. "We're soaking wet, you've got no weapon..." He glanced around as if something had dawned on him. "Neither have I. I have absolutely no idea when I lost that."

"We can't just leave them."

"I'm not saying that, but we're no good unarmed, either. Let's go back to the truck first. Jack and the others will head that way, too. If they're not there, we can find something else to use as a weapon and come back."

He didn't sound like he was totally thrilled with the idea, but Violet knew he wouldn't leave their friends behind.

"Okay," she agreed. She opened the door, and the two of them stepped into the dark hallway beyond. Joe unzipped his backpack and took out his flashlight.

"Where are we?" Violet asked as they began to walk.

He glanced into one of the rooms they were passing. "They're offices. Jack said he checked them yesterday." He pointed to a bend in the hallway up ahead. "I bet that takes us to the lobby—there was a door out there that said Staff Only."

"Great, then we—"

Joe held out his hand, stopping her. She heard it, too—zombie screams. They were coming.

Seconds later, someone skidded around the corner up ahead as though the floor were greased. It was a small, skinny man, who waved his hands wildly at the pair of them, too out of breath to make any noise. A wave of zombies followed him, blocking the exit. The man hit the floor, whether from losing his footing or from sheer exhaustion they couldn't tell, and the creatures fell upon him. But there were so many, and while a few began to feast on his body, the rest hurtled past, Violet and Joe clearly in their sights.

Joe pushed open a door to their right, and the pair of them hurried inside.

"No lock. Typical." He held the door closed as the biters arrived. "Find something to keep it shut!"

Violet spun around, damp hair clinging to her fore-head. There was a desk by the window. She tried to drag it, but it was too heavy. She grabbed hold of the comput-er monitor and shoved it onto the floor, along with all the other things littering the surface, then tried to move the desk again. It was still incredibly heavy, but slowly she was able to pull it across the room to Joe. She felt several of her nails rip off, and sweat poured from every place on her body it was possible to sweat from, but at last she was close enough for him to grab hold of one end and help maneuver it into place. It kept the door closed, and though the dead still pounded on the other side, they couldn't get in. For now.

For a moment Violet and Joe stood and watched the shaking door. Her mouth was dry, and the back of her throat burned. As she tried to catch her breath, she al-lowed herself a minute to think about Jack and the others. Where were they? Had they managed to get away from the biters? Or were they floating face down in the pool with the other bodies?

Then she smelled it.

Blood.

It was fresh, but different. This blood was changing. Someone was turning. Right now, in that very room. Joe sensed it, too, and he looked around anxiously. There was a body on the floor not far from where the desk had been. It was a woman. Violet didn't know how she had missed her before. The woman's eyes were closed. Her arm was a gory mess, bitten in too many places to count. She was twitching.

More banging from the door. The biters weren't going anywhere, and now Violet and Joe were trapped.

The woman's eyes flicked open, and she took a long, dry, rasping breath. Her copper hair, matted and stained with blood, curtained her face as she slowly got to her feet. The movements were jerky, like a movie which had been poorly cut together. Her face whipped in the direction of the door, and she regarded Joe and Violet with an expres-sion that changed from blank disinterest, to curiosity, to anger, all within the space of mere seconds.

Both of their hands were painfully empty. Violet's eyes swept the room frantically for anything they could use to kill the biter. Nothing. The computer screen hadn't been very heavy, and it'd broken into pieces which were now behind the woman anyway. The only other things in the room were books, the desk chair, and a couple of filing cabinets. The creature stumbled toward them clumsily. Biters were always slow for the first few minutes after reanimating, but that would change quickly. Joe grabbed the desk chair, held it up, and ran at the zombie, using it to pin her against the wall. She fought back, already strong. Violet rushed to the window, their only escape option, and tried to wrench it open. It was locked.

"It won't move," she cried, searching the windowsill for the key but finding nothing.

"Smash it," Joe groaned, working hard to hold the woman back. She snapped her jaws hungrily. Violet couldn't see anything in the room strong enough to shatter the glass. Her heart raced. She charged to the desk, pulling open the drawers and hurriedly shuffling through the things inside.

"Any day now," Joe puffed as the biter pushed against the chair.

Violet found the key, crying out with excitement. "I've got it!"

"Fantastic."

She rushed to the window, unlocked it, and slid the large pane to the side. The sky, so clear earlier, was blanketed with dark clouds, and heavy rain poured. The back of the building was at the edge of a steep slope. With the rain turning the ground to mud, Violet wasn't sure she would be able to remain upright when she got outside.

"It's really steep."

"Oh no, do you want to stay here instead?" Joe called sarcastically, struggling to hold the dead woman in place. The door beside him shifted, the desk inching away and allowing rotting fingers to curl around the sides

"Go," Joe ordered, fighting back as the woman pushed against the chair, arms swiping at him aggressively. "I'll drop her as soon as you're gone."

Another squeak as the desk moved again—now whole hands and arms were reaching through the opening. Violet could hear the hungry cries of the biters. She took a breath, then climbed out of the window and onto the steep bank. She had guessed right; from the moment her feet touched the muddy ground, she slipped and slid the entire way from the window to the bottom of the slope, a journey of at least forty feet. Rocks, sticks, and other sharp objects tore the back of her shirt and pierced her skin.

Finally, she stopped sliding and lay still for a moment in the mud. The cold rain pattering down on her face was soothing, but she only allowed herself a couple of seconds to enjoy it. She needed to check out the damage to her back from the slide down as well as her arms, which had also been scratched up. She chanced a peek, but it wasn't too bad. Not about to bleed out any time soon, anyway. Slowly, she sat up, glancing back up the slope at the window.

Joe should've climbed out by now.
Don't panic. You'll see his face any second.
Then she heard the scream.

AS SOON AS SHE HEARD THE SCREAM, VIOLET BEGAN to climb back up the muddy slope. *Not again,* she told herself. She refused to leave another friend behind. Unfortunately, trying to make her way up the slippery mud bank was practically impossible. Each time she gained a foot or two, she slid back down again. The rain continued to pour, and every slip spattered her with more mud. It was in her mouth, up her arms, and caked in her hair, but she wouldn't give up. She couldn't. Not with Joe still up there. He couldn't get infected, but he could still die. She would not allow herself to lose another friend.

Violet gritted her teeth and forced herself on, digging her hands into the soft mud right up to her knuckles in an attempt to gain a grip. It worked, and finally she began to make headway. In fact, she was almost halfway up the hill when Joe collided with her on his way down. They tumbled and slid over the wet ground until they landed uncomfortably at the base of the slope. For a minute or two, the pair simply lay in the mud, the rain hammering down on their filthy faces.

"Hi," Violet eventually exhaled.

"How's it going?"

"I was waiting for you."

"Sorry, you know how women are. She wouldn't

S

E

V

E

N

let me leave."

Violet grinned, then sat up, examining herself. Any places she had managed to avoid getting muddy on her initial journey down the slope had been much less fortunate on the second trip.

"I don't look great," she muttered, wiping her arm across her filthy shirt.

"I've got you beat," Joe said, still on his back. Violet tilted her head to one side, about to ask how, when she saw the new bite on his shoulder. It was the opposite side to where he had first been bitten all those months ago. And while it wasn't a death sentence for him, it was still not exactly something to show off. If anyone but Violet had seen it, Joe would probably have an axe in his skull right now. For the first time that day, she was grateful they were alone and leaned in to inspect the wound more closely. It was ugly, but not too deep. A few drops of blood trickled out slowly.

"It's not so bad," she said. "Barely even broke the skin."

Joe finally sat up, adjusting his ripped shirt to cover the wound. "Yeah. But it ruins my dreams of being a shoulder model."

Violet felt the corners of her mouth twitch. She shuffled closer and kissed Joe once on the cheek. She wasn't usually one for outward displays of affection, so followed this action up with a gentle shove. "I thought you were dead. I heard you scream."

"Well yeah, it hurt."

"At least you're alive."

Joe shrugged. "As much as the two of us can be, anyway." He got to his feet, holding out his hand to help her up, too.

Violet decided he was right—he definitely had it a lot worse than she did. Not only was he bitten, but his shoulder and lip were also bleeding, and his posture suggested he was practically ready to drop from exhaustion. Like her, he was covered in mud, as well as green slime from their dip in the pool. "You're no oil painting, either," he said with a weak smile, as if he could read her mind. "We should get going. I killed the one up there, but the biters were almost through the door. I'd rather not have to deal with twenty of those things sliding down the hill."

Violet nodded. "We need to go around to the front. That's where the truck and cars are."

"That's a terrible idea. Those zombies had to have come through the front door; there was no other way in. We can't be sure there aren't even more of them waiting for us." He gestured to the woods not far from where they stood. "We should cut through the woods and take the long way back to the road. We can wait for the truck there."

"Jack and the others will go to the truck. If we don't make it back soon, they'll think we're dead. They'll leave us behind."

Joe didn't seem convinced.

"It's our only option," Violet pressed. "We can't just wait around for the truck in hopes it passes. We need to see if they're still here."

"You're asking me to trust you?"

"Yes."

"Even though I'm still bleeding from the last time I did?"

"It was your idea to jump out the window!"

"But it was your idea to go into the building in the first place. If we'd stayed in the truck, we would've been dry, armed, and not slowly bleeding out."

She narrowed her gaze. "Let's not get overdramatic. Come on." She turned, squelching through the mud toward a place where the ground leveled out. It took a while, the building was huge, and navigating around it over slippery terrain resulted in Violet stumbling more than once. She didn't know how long they had been walking, only that the rain had stopped by the time she and Joe peered around the side of the building. There were no zombies, but the truck and car were gone.

Joe swore, leaning back against the wall.

"At least it means they're alive," Violet muttered.

"Yeah, because that's what I was worrying about," he replied, pressing a palm to the bite on his shoulder. It had stopped bleeding at least. "What are we going to do?"

"We'll have to walk."

"Great."

And so, they began the long walk back to Harmony. Violet had no idea how long it would take on foot, particularly in wet clothes. She tried to tell herself it could've been worse, but she found it didn't provide much comfort.

AN HOUR LATER, THE PAIR OF THEM HAD ALMOST COMpletely dried out, so instead of being wet, dirty, and exhausted, they were just dirty and exhausted. It didn't feel like a huge improvement.

"I think you look great."

Matt's voice again. This was from a few days before the warehouse. He'd been smiling at Violet after the pair of them had fought off four corpses. She'd glanced down at herself, an eyebrow raised.

"Matt, I'm literally covered in blood."

"...It's your color."

Violet shook her head. Why was she remembering these things now? Why was Matt at the forefront of her mind after she'd refused to allow herself to even think of his name for so long?

Joe spotted something up ahead, and he hurried toward the half-eaten remains of a corpse just beyond a burned-out car.

"What is it?" Violet asked, wishing more than ever that she had a weapon. She watched anxiously as Joe reached down and grabbed something. It was a hat. An incredibly ugly hat. It was turquoise, and trimmed in bright red. He brushed some dirt from the surface and then put it on. Turning around, he flashed Violet a winning smile. "What do you think?"

"I think it's a hat."

"Isn't it great?"

"I mean... it's turquoise."

Joe shook his head. "It's not just turquoise. It's a turquoise *fedora*. You don't see those around."

"I can't imagine why not."

He winked. "Our luck is changing."

No sooner had the words left his lips than the smile was wiped from his face. His eyes focused on something over Violet's shoulder. She froze where she stood, heart racing.

"Is it zombies?" she asked quietly, not daring to turn.

Joe shook his head. "No."

She allowed herself to breathe. "Oh good."

"It's lions."

Never relax until you hear the end of the sentence, Violet.

Turning slowly, she saw six female lions watching them from around thirty meters away.

"This is okay, right?" Joe asked quietly. "The big guy isn't here. They're probably not looking for food."

Violet shook her head. "The males don't hunt. The females hunt."

"Wonderful."

"I think we should go."

"I think so, too."

Slowly, they began to back away. Joe reached for Violet's hand. The lions were moving now, padding toward them silently. The cats took their time, as if they were in no hurry at all.

Maybe they don't want to eat us. Maybe they're simply curious.

Yeah, and maybe they're licking their lips out of curiosity.

"Should we run?" Joe asked.

"I don't know." Violet turned and stopped in her tracks. Two more female lions were only fifteen meters behind them.

"They're boxing us in," Joe said.

Violet spotted a store to their right. They could make it if they ran. And if the door was unlocked. And if they were fast. Probably.

Joe followed her gaze. "Remember, you don't have to be faster than them."

"I only have to be faster than you."

"Exactly. Go!"

They broke into a run, charging for the safety of the

store at full speed. Violet could hear movement as the lions began to run, but she and Joe were almost there. They were going to make it. She shoved the door open, then threw herself inside. Joe slammed it shut as the first lion arrived. It jumped, standing up on its hind legs as its claws slipped across the glass. Joe turned the lock, and it clicked into place.

Violet backed up, trying to catch her breath.

It's okay. You're safe now. You're sa—

She screamed as a zombie grabbed hold of her arms from behind, snapping its teeth just an inch from her ear. Joe practically flew over, tackling the dead man and forcing him to let go. The biter fell to the floor, and Joe smashed his foot into the creature's head. The brittle skull caved in, and the thing stopped moving.

Joe stumbled back, panting heavily.

"Wow," Violet panted. "You stomped on his head."

"Yeah."

"That's pretty hardcore."

"Did it look tough?"

"A bit."

"Was it impressive?"

"Don't get excited."

Joe grinned, and Violet took a step closer. "Thanks."

He waved his hand as if to say it was nothing, then glanced around. "Let's see if there's anything useful here."

They searched the store, but it had clearly been looted many times over the past year. There was barely anything left that wasn't nailed down. There was no food, no water, and nothing that could work as a weapon. Violet found some sugar-free gum under the counter, Joe discovered a box of matches, and that was it. The whole time they searched, the lions remained outside. Most of them were sitting or lying down, but a couple were pacing, eyes fixed on the two sacks of fresh meat inside.

"We should find a back way out," Joe said. "They're just going to wait for us."

"Okay," Violet agreed, "but I need to use the bathroom first." In reality, she didn't want to leave just yet. Joe still looked worse for wear, and she wanted to give him at least a couple more minutes to rest before they got moving again.

He hauled himself up onto the countertop while she headed through a door at the back of the store. It led to an employee lounge, which had been cleared of anything useful a long time ago. There was a back door at the far end of the room, and she chanced a glance out the little window. No lions in sight. This would be their best exit.

There was another door, which Violet assumed would be for the bathroom, but when she opened it, she found a narrow staircase leading up. She paused at the bottom step, hand resting on the cracked wooden handle. Calling back to Joe and asking him to come up with her would probably be the most sensible choice, but he was beat and didn't need to trudge up a flight of stairs to help her explore what would almost certainly be a couple of empty rooms. The two of them had been in the store for a while; if there were any biters upstairs, they would've surely heard them by now.

She took a breath and headed up. The wooden floorboards creaked loudly underfoot, but there were no sounds of movement from this floor. She stepped out onto a narrow hallway. There were two doors to her right, and one to her left. She opened that one first and found the bathroom. It was small, dingy, and probably hadn't been an altogether pleasant place even before a year of abandonment. The dirty toilet seat hung unevenly from a single screw. The sink was stained and contained a small pile of what appeared to be chicken bones. As Violet entered the room, dozens of small bugs scuttled away into dark corners. She closed the door with a grimace, frowning at the fact that even the toilet paper had been looted.

Let's get this over with.

When she was done, she took a peek out of the filthy window. She could just about see the street below, but not the front door. It didn't matter; the lions were probably still there. She doubted they would give up so easily, especially when they could still see Joe through the glass door. The pair of them would definitely have to sneak out the back. She just had to hope they could get far enough away before the animals decided to explore a little further.

There were footsteps on the staircase outside the bathroom door. Joe must've been coming upstairs to take a look around.

"Nothing in here," she called. "I'll be right out." She checked the cabinet above the sink. No pain killers, no bandages. Just a single box of laxatives.

Is that something I should grab?

If anything, running from zombies all day keeps you pretty regular.

Joe knocked.

"Hang on," Violet muttered. She opened the door with a smile, shaking the box of laxatives. "Do you need these?"

But it wasn't Joe.

E I G H T

THE MAN IN FRONT OF HER WAS TALL AND SKINNY, wearing tattered clothes stained with blood and dirt. His hair was brown and shoulder length, hanging lank and filthy at his shoulders. His brown eyes were sunken into his gaunt face, as though he hadn't eaten in weeks. He was holding a knife. He smiled, revealing two rows of crumbling yellow teeth. "Hello there."

There's blood on his knife.

Whose blood is that?

At first, Violet did nothing. She felt as though someone had squeezed the air out of her lungs. The pounding of her heart sounded like a drum, so loud she was sure he could hear it.

Then, the moment passed. She made to slam the door shut, but the man was faster and wrenched it open with ease. She started to yell Joe's name, but the stranger slapped his dirty hand over her mouth. He placed his knife to her throat, forcing her back against the doorframe. "Don't make a sound." Slowly he ran his nose along her neck, inhaling deeply. Violet felt her stomach turn over.

The blood on his knife didn't make her turn. Was that because it belonged to a zombie? Joe's blood didn't tempt her, either—it could just as easily be his.

These thoughts raced through her head in the few seconds she and the stranger stood in silence, staring at one another. Her eyes were wide and frightened; his, determined. Then, with one swift move, he pulled her out of the bathroom and dragged her down the hallway. She struggled, but it made no difference. Despite being so thin, the man was surprisingly strong. He kicked open the door in front of him and shoved her into the room and onto a filthy mattress on the floor. It was stained with blood and other things that Violet didn't want to imagine. He moved back over to the door, closing it softly. She felt as though there was a weight on top of her, preventing her from getting up or even making a sound.

She could see him more clearly now, thanks to the light pouring through the smashed window. He was probably only a few years older than she was, but he'd clearly been having a tougher zompocalypse. He definitely hadn't eaten a decent meal in a long time, and even though she was sitting on a mattress that she was fairly sure had been used as a toilet, the most overpowering smell in the room was actually coming from his dirt-encrusted skin and rancid clothing. He raised a bony finger to his cracked lips. "Keep quiet, and I won't have to slice you up first."

'First'?

"Did you hurt my friend?" Violet whispered. She didn't seem able to make her voice any louder.

The man grinned. "*I* didn't hurt him. But my friend? I can't speak for him. We made a deal when we heard you—I get the girl, he gets the boy. He likes boys, I like girls."

Despite the implications of his statement, Violet felt her muscles relax just a fraction. It wasn't Joe's blood. This man hadn't hurt him. But her friend was still downstairs with someone dangerous, and she was trapped up here. As if on cue, there were sounds from downstairs. Joe cried out, and she could hear things being knocked over.

The stranger was still smiling. "The girls are always easier, but hey, you want who you want, right? No judgements here."

Violet's heart was beating painfully fast. Her face was hot, and beads of sweat pricked on her forehead. It was as though the world around her had slowed down. The man was talking again, but his voice sounded so far away that the words hardly made sense. Her brain, however, had sped up, and a barrage of questions raced through her mind. Was Joe dead? If not, how long would that be true for? What would this man do to her?

Suddenly her captor's voice broke through. "You keep quiet, and I won't hurt you."

That's a lie.

Still holding the knife, he reached with his free hand to unbuckle his belt and took a single step closer. "You going to be good?" he asked.

Violet nodded.

See, I can lie, too.

"Good." He took another step closer. Violet kept her eyes fixed on his, not even daring to blink. She wouldn't let him see that she was afraid. She wouldn't give him the satisfaction.

Just a little bit closer. Go on, I dare you.

You want to know what happened to the last man who tried this?

He took another step. Violet head-butted him, hitting him squarely in the stomach. Swearing loudly, he staggered back and slashed wildly with the knife. She got to her feet as he swung in her direction, managing to jump aside just before it contacted her face. He lost his footing—mostly because his jeans had slipped down and become tangled around his legs—but the rabid, half-dressed man was still determinedly swinging a knife at her. He slashed violently in her direction again, and Violet used her arm to knock the weapon out of his hand. She ran to the door, grabbed the handle, and wrenched it open, but the stranger was too close, taking hold of her by the shoulder as she passed and ramming her head into the wood. The pain was blinding, and she stumbled back as the world around her became momentarily white. He pushed her down onto the mattress with a groan. She couldn't seem to pull herself upright, and though she could see him in front of her, she was unable to focus on his face.

"Now," he panted, picking up the knife from the floor, "now I'm gonna make it hurt."

As he took a step closer, the door swung open behind him. Joe was bleeding from his side, but he was alive. He launched himself at the man, knocking him to the ground. The knife slid along the floor. The two men fought, Joe with his hands around the stranger's neck, the stranger punching Joe's face. Violet wanted to get up, wanted to help, but her head still throbbed painfully, and she felt a trickle of warm liquid on her forehead. Joe yelped as the man punched him in the stomach where his shirt was already stained with blood.

Do something!

The words echoed in Violet's mind, and she did as she was told, rolling onto her side and crawling across the floor to grab the knife. She got shakily to her feet. The stranger was now on top of Joe, his hands locked tightly around her friend's neck. Charging across the room, Violet slammed the blade into the man's back.

She only half-considered the consequences of her actions. All she'd been thinking about was getting the guy off Joe, but the second his blood began to pour, the room started to spin.

Oh yeah. This.

WHEN VIOLET WOKE UP, THE ROOM HAD DARKENED. Through the broken window she could see the sun sinking toward the horizon. She was on her back on the floor, the familiar smell of drying blood all around her. The taste in her mouth told her that she had definitely fed, but she didn't feel all too guilty about it.

Slowly she sat up, looking around. Joe was sitting on the filthy bed, blood around his mouth, down the front of his shirt, and on his hands. He caught her eye and gave a weak smile.

"Good sleep?"

"The usual." She glanced over at what was left of the man. His stomach, neck and arms had been thoroughly feasted on. Uncomfortably full and bloated, she crawled over to Joe on her hands and knees, then pulled herself into a sitting position on the mattress beside him. "Show me," she said, pointing to his stomach.

He lifted his shirt. The wound wasn't actually that bad—more of a slash than a stab.

"Did you kill him?" Violet asked.

Joe nodded. "I jammed his knife into his ear, but I ran before I lost control. I had to get to you... He told me what his friend wanted—"

"It's okay," she interrupted, putting her hand on his arm and taking a deep breath. "I thought he was going to kill you."

"So did I. Turns out, he knew even less about using a knife than I do. He's ruined my six pack, though." He'd clearly gone back downstairs as he was once more wearing the hideous fedora. Violet pulled it off and hit him with it before flinging the hat across the room.

He raised an eyebrow. "I understand you're emotional, but what do you have against my hat?"

"You scared me! I thought you were..." She trailed off, not even wanting to finish the thought, let alone hear the words aloud.

"Sorry, Vi." He grimaced slightly, clearly still in considerable pain.

"We should go back," she began, looking at the window.

Joe shook his head. "That seems like a terrible idea. It'll be dark soon."

"We can't be that far away. We should make it in an hour or so. Or, I suppose, we have to spend the night here."

His eyes flicked to the corpse on the floor. "Actually, I fancy a walk."

Violet hadn't realized how dark it was getting until she opened the back door. There was a good chance they wouldn't get home before night fell. The lions, at least, were nowhere in sight. All was quiet.

Too quiet.

Don't do that. Why are you doing that?

Violet jumped as something grabbed hold of her shoulders. She spun and shoved Joe, who'd purposefully tried to scare her.

"Why would you do that?"

He grinned, shrugging. "I don't know, you just looked so serious."

Violet widened her eyes, speaking in an angry whisper. "It *is* serious! There are zombies out here! And lions! And, as we've just seen, maniac rapists!"

He scanned their surroundings casually. "I can't see any now, though."

"Do you ever take anything seriously?"

He stroked his chin thoughtfully, as if really considering the question. "Do you think I should grow a beard?"

Violet rolled her eyes. "Come on, let's go."

They began to walk, and after a few moments of silence, Joe spoke quietly. "To be honest, it's less about whether I *should* grow a beard and more about whether I *could* grow a beard. Maurice here took some real work."

"I really wish you'd stop calling it that."

"It took ages to get it how I wanted. Do you remember when it was all patchy?"

"Who could forget?"

They walked for twenty minutes, and Joe continued to ponder his facial-hair possibilities as darkness drew over them.

"I just think it sort of legitimizes a man, you know?"

"Mm-hmm."

"You see a guy with a beard, and it's just like, *there's* a man who knows what he wants."

"What does he want?"

"Well... I guess he wanted a beard, and now he has one."

"That's not really reaching for the stars though, is it?"

Before Violet could say any more, Joe held his arm across her chest, forcing her to stop walking.

"What?" she asked, straining to see whatever had caught his eye. It was dark, but she could just make out movement in the distance. "What is it? The lions?" Her heart began to hammer, but Joe shook his head.

"No, not lions."

"Oh, thank God for that."

"Zombies."

74

She could see them now, and worse still, they had seen her. The creatures began to run. She didn't know how many there were, but it was more than she could count on two hands.

"This way," Joe said, turning down a narrow gap between the two buildings to their left. It was even darker down there, and Violet instinctively held her hands out as she ran, only just able to make out the shape of him in front of her.

"In here!"

Someone was calling to them, and Violet could see a figure in a doorway up ahead.

Please don't be a maniac rapist. Please don't be a maniac rapist.

Even just a maniac would be better.

They didn't have time to discuss it, charging desperately into the building. The stranger slammed the door behind them, then hurried through a door to the right before either of them could even speak to him. Violet heard him heading up some stairs. She and Joe followed; it wasn't like they had many other choices. Not with the dead so close.

As they entered the room at the top of the stairs, she could see the man over by the window. There was a single candle burning in the corner of the bedroom, and in the dim light she saw it had been ransacked. There was garbage everywhere, and the walls were heavily graffitied. The man kept his face turned away, focusing his attention on the window.

"They didn't see you come in," he muttered. "You're safe now."

Joe grabbed Violet's arm, squeezing it tightly. Her head swam. She knew that voice, too.

It was Matt.

VIOLET FLUNG HERSELF INTO MATT'S ARMS WITH such force that he was knocked backward.

This isn't real, this can't be happening, Matt was dead. Matt is dead.

But she knew that voice anywhere, and now, holding onto him tightly, felt the familiar weight of his arms around her. His heartbeat, as familiar as her own, was hammering against her chest. Matt was alive.

"I thought I'd never see you again," she choked, finally releasing her hold and taking a step back. Joe pulled his flashlight out of his bag and shone it at Matt's face.

He looks different.

Other than the squint—which Violet assumed was due to the light shining directly in his eyes rather than some kind of recent eye injury—there were several changes to Matt's physical appearance. His dark brown hair was longer and even more untidy than usual. His green eyes had lost their spark and were ringed with dark circles, as though it had been a long time since he'd slept. It was his expression, though, which seemed most unusual. If Violet had been in shock, Matt appeared even more so. He seemed to be in complete disbelief, as though waiting for the punchline of a cruel joke.

**N
I
N
E**

"What's wrong?" Violet asked.

Matt shook his head. "I... this can't be real. They told me you were dead."

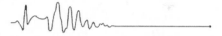

MATT KNEW THIS WAS A BAD IDEA, AND THOUGH HE TRIED to ignore the thought it repeated itself over and over in his head, immune to his attempts to suffocate it. They had not expected to find other survivors in the warehouse, and though they had agreed to an uneasy truce, he couldn't shake the feeling that something terrible was about to happen. He glanced to his left, where Toby walked beside him with a fixed expression on his face. The boy looked up at Matt, his eyes said, 'I know, I feel it, too.'

They rounded the corner, and that's when they found them, more biters than Matt had seen clustered together in a long time. For a moment, the four survivors froze, eyes fixed on the dead. The zombies were all standing still like mannequins. However, as soon as one of them saw Matt and the others, it screamed. Within seconds, the whole horde was charging toward the group.

The man called Neil had a gun and began firing at the wave of running corpses. It made little difference. The biters were getting closer. Neil glanced at Matt and Toby, made eye contact for less than a second, and then fired a single shot into Matt's leg. He grabbed the hand of the woman he was with, and the two of them fled.

The searing pain from the bullet caused Matt to stumble back, but he managed to stay upright, grabbing hold of his leg immediately and trying to apply pressure as blood poured from the wound. He knew there was no way he'd be able to put enough weight on it to escape the dead.

"Run," he ordered Toby, who ignored him completely, taking Matt's arm and slinging it over his own shoulder. Whether it was adrenaline or a high pain threshold he'd never known about, Matt was able to keep up the pace for a while, and together the two of them ran back toward the main doors. As they rounded a corner, Toby released his hold and pulled a shelving unit down on the biters, though

it did little to slow them down. The pain in Matt's leg became even more agonizing, and now that he had stopped running, he felt sure he was about to black out. Toby rejoined him, and Matt managed to go on a little farther, but it was no good. He could see Violet and Joe, standing near the door. He knew neither of them could come to help him. One sniff of the blood and they would lose control. He was glad. He didn't want his friends to risk their lives for him. None of them. He glanced over his shoulder; the dead were getting closer. He had to do it now.

He pushed Toby away. "Run!" he instructed. "I can't make it. Go!"

Toby shook his head, grabbing Matt's arm once more.

Matt dislodged him again. "Go! Don't die here, go!"

The boy looked helpless and made one last attempt to pull Matt onwards, but he refused to move. Finally, the kid turned and ran to his friends. Matt felt a wave of relief rush over him, leaning on the nearby shelf for support. His eyes found Violet once more. She was crying; he could see the blood streaking down her beautiful face. He only wished—

His feet were pulled out from beneath him, and he heard Violet's scream a second before his head hit the concrete, hard. Everything took on a soft focus as he was dragged under the shelving. The biters were trying to grab his hands and pull him back, piling on top of each other so high that he lost all sight of anything but their dead flesh, but he was being dragged to safety beneath the shelving unit and away from them. He could still hear the screaming in the distance, but he was no longer sure who it was.

Then there was another scream from someone close beside him, and everything went dark.

MATT WOKE UP A FEW DAYS LATER IN A BED HE DIDN'T recognize, being watched by a man he didn't know.

"I wasn't sure you'd ever wake up," the stranger said, blowing cigarette smoke out of the open window next to him. He took another drag and then stubbed it out. "How *are you feeling?" He had a thick Irish accent and a friend-ly face.*

Matt reached up to touch his head. It was sore, heavy, but still attached. "Okay," he muttered. "Where am I?"

"Somewhere safe." The man stepped over to the side of the bed and held out his hand to Matt. "I'm Luke."

"Matt."

"You took a pretty hard whack when you went down. I was starting to worry." Luke cocked his head to one side. "What do you remember?"

Matt thought for a moment, the memories came back in fragments. "The warehouse, being shot, my friends—" Suddenly, it all fell into place, and he struggled to get to his feet. Pain seared through his leg, and he stumbled back into a sitting position. "What happened to my friends?"

"They're dead."

That was woman's voice, and Matt watched her come into the room. She must've been about eighteen or nine-teen. She was tall, very slender, and with chestnut hair tied high on her head. She regarded Matt as though he were something on the bottom of her shoe, but he didn't care about that. He was reeling from her words and shook his aching head.

"No, they can't be. They were by the door. They were supposed to get out..."

"We saw them go down," Luke said. "All of them, ripped to bits. When we carried you outside to the car, they were being torn up." He lowered his head. "I'm sorry. We couldn't help them."

"Just like we couldn't help James," the woman said coldly.

"Anna," Luke began, his voice gentle, "you know that's not Matt's fault—"

"James died helping us pull Matt out," Anna spat, step-ping closer. "He got grabbed and ripped apart because you were so concerned with trying to help him." She stabbed her finger in Matt's direction.

Luke sighed, rubbing his temples. "James wanted to help just as much as I did. Don't blame Matt for this."

Anna waved her hand in exasperation and stomped

out of the room. Luke turned his attention back to the bed.

"She doesn't mean it. She's just upset. It's been us and James for a while."

"My friends are dead?" Matt's head was swimming. "I just can't..."

"I'm sorry."

"You're sure?"

Luke nodded. "I saw it. I can take you there when you're better, if you want, but to be honest there probably won't be much left."

"Three of them?" Matt persisted. "A kid, a guy about my age, and..." he couldn't even bring himself to ask about Violet. How could he describe her in a single sentence?

Luke's nod was like an ice pick in Matt's chest. "I didn't see the boy go down, but I saw the parts that were left. I guess they got him first. I saw the other two, though."

Matt's brain was a scramble, and he found himself murmuring, "What about the dog? Did you see the dog?"

Luke shook his head. "No. No dog. Sorry." He reached out, squeezing Matt's arm gently. "I'm truly sorry for the people you lost. I know it probably doesn't mean anything now, but I'd really like you to stay with us. We can keep you safe. No one should be on their own out there, not anymore."

Alone. That was what he was now. The realization settled over Matt like a blanket of needles. He was alone.

AFTER ALMOST TWO WEEKS, MATT WAS FIT ENOUGH TO start walking around, supported by a stick. He insisted on being taken back to the cottage where he had lived with Violet and the others. Anna hadn't been keen.

"What's the point?" she asked, leaning against the kitchen counter of the house they were holed up in. "We saw them die, they're not going to be there waiting for you."

"Anna," Luke began softly but firmly.

She shrugged. "What? It's the truth. He's deluding himself if he thinks going there will make him feel better."

Matt was starting to realize that Anna had a habit of

talking about him as though he weren't there. Not that he really cared.

"It's not that," he interrupted. "There are some things I need to get." The excuse was poor, Anna and Luke knew as well as he did that he was still in denial. Despite what they had said about seeing his friends getting ripped apart, he would not be able to believe it until he went home. Maybe not even then.

"Please," he insisted.

Anna rolled her eyes. "Whatever."

They went to the warehouse first, but there was nothing to see. Most of the blood had been washed away after several days of heavy rain. The bodies, ripped apart as they were and scattered across the parking lot, had been picked clean by biters, birds, and other scavenging animals. Matt could never hope to identify what was left. The truck was gone, but that meant nothing. It had probably been stolen over the past few weeks. They'd left the keys inside, after all.

Several hours later, they arrived at the cottage. Luke and Anna went in first since Matt was still leaning heavily on the stick when walking and had little hope of defending himself against any biters who may have gotten inside. As he approached the front door, watching the two of them disappear through it, he had no idea what he was expecting. Did he really think he would find Joe and Violet sitting at the kitchen table? Or Toby playing with Ben on the floor?

No, he was fairly sure that wasn't going to happen, but still, that didn't mean his stomach didn't drop when he entered his old home and found it exactly as it had been when they'd left almost two weeks ago. Their plates from breakfast were sitting on the draining board. The tennis ball Toby used to throw for Ben was waiting idly on the floor by the table. The crude cartoon Joe had drawn the morning they left was still tacked to the fridge. Jack and Anna re-entered the kitchen.

"There's no one here," Jack said quietly.

Matt nodded, the only response he felt capable of.

"Do you want to get your belongings?" Jack asked.

"No, let's just go."

FROM THEN ON, MATT, LUKE, AND ANNA KEPT EACH OTHER *alive. Matt liked Luke because he didn't talk much. He was quick, good at getting into places for supplies, and normally able to put a positive spin on the most dire of situations. Luke liked Matt because he was strong, clever, and didn't complain about anything. He might not have been one for long conversations, but neither was Luke, and that was something they had in common at least.*

Matt soon discovered Anna wasn't so bad, either, and after a few weeks she even began to talk to him like he was a human being. She and Luke had apparently found each other a few months before the warehouse and began a relationship not long after that. Matt didn't know what kept them together as they had little in common, but whatever it was, it was working at least. The three of them kept each other safe for months, and all seemed to be going swimmingly well.

Until Luke got bitten.

It was quick. None of them realized it had happened at first. They were in a house searching for supplies. They didn't know the biters were inside until Matt opened a door and four of them came out. It wasn't like they couldn't handle four—they'd killed more than that on numerous occasions. But for some reason, that time was different. Later, Matt would try to dissect every minute of their time in that house, trying to work out what he could've changed. But in reality, there was nothing. One minute they were fine, the next they were fighting, and the next the biters were dead. Matt had been struggling with one of them, and Luke had pulled it from him. That must've been the one that got him, though they didn't see it happen. It was only when the fighting was all over that Matt saw the bite.

He said nothing, just stared at Luke's bloody arm as though hypnotized. Luke followed his gaze, and then so did Anna.

"Damn," Luke breathed. He looked up at Matt, shrug-

ging his shoulders. "One of those things," he murmured. The three of them remained frozen on the spot for several moments, then Luke sighed, handing Matt his axe.

Anna moved closer, shaking her head. "No. No, no, no, no, no."

"You know what has to happen," Luke whispered.

"No. No, we can do something. We..." she trailed off, a choking sob rising in her throat.

Luke held out his arms, and she collapsed into them, silent tears streaming down her cheeks. He soothed her quietly, then whispered something in her ear. For a moment, her sobs became louder, but slowly she released her hold on him and stepped back. She went over to the window, not looking at either of them. Luke motioned to the axe. Matt shook his head, trying to give it back, but Luke wouldn't take it. "Come on, you know you have to."

"I can't."

"Please." Luke lowered his voice, which cracked when he spoke. "I can't do it myself." His eyes flicked to Anna. "I can't make her do it, either, and I don't want to be one of those things."

Matt knew he didn't have a choice. He owed Luke that much. It was all his fault. Just like it was with James, who'd died saving him from the biters. Just like it was with Violet, Joe, and Toby, because the warehouse had been his idea, after all. It was always Matt's fault when people died. The least he could do was this one thing.

Luke got onto his knees. "Good luck." His eyes flicked to Anna once more. "Take care of her," he whispered.

Matt raised the axe, then brought it down on Luke's head.

"I WAS SO SURE YOU GUYS WERE..." MATT TRAILED OFF. "Luke said he saw you die."

Joe shook his head. "He must've seen the others, those people we met in the warehouse. We saw them fighting the dead outside, but we were already in the truck when they went down. I don't know why they didn't drive away when they got the chance. I guess they didn't want to give the place up."

"I went back to the cottage," Matt continued, shaking his head. "You weren't there, you hadn't been back at all."

"None of us wanted to go back," Joe said, lowering his voice. "It didn't feel right, not without you. We just drove for hours. Finally, we found this old house at the edge of town and stopped there. I don't know how long for."

Violet remembered those days, the long silences, the glazed looks they all wore. She hadn't eaten, she'd barely slept, and after a while her life started to feel like a hazy dream. If Ezra's people hadn't found them, she truly wondered if she, Joe, and Toby would ever have managed to bring themselves back to reality. Slowly, over the following months, they had learned to cope with losing Matt. They didn't talk about it, and she imagined that, like herself, the other two didn't even let themselves think about it. But they had learned to go on, at least.

Yet here Matt was, sitting on the floor opposite them, skinny and tired but very much alive.

"I'm sorry," he said, eyes lowered. "That must've been—"

"Don't be sorry," Joe interrupted. "You were going through the same thing."

"Is Toby okay?"

"He's fine. He's safe at home. Even the dog made it."

Relief flooded Matt's face, and his features softened. He was suddenly the same Matt he had always been, and something warm settled in Violet's stomach. It was a comfortable feeling, almost like slipping into a pair of old shoes. She hadn't been able to speak yet, still trying to wrap her head around everything, and was mildly aware that her mouth was open in a less-than-attractive expression. There were a million things she knew she should say, but the words stuck in her throat like cement. None of them felt like enough, anyway.

"Matt..." she began, her voice little more than a whisper. "We thought... We saw..."

Joe came to her rescue. "If we'd thought there was any chance you were alive—"

"I know," Matt interrupted. "I feel the same. I can't believe it's been so long."

He was right. They'd been apart longer than they'd been together. Much longer. Yet so much of Violet's life since the dead had started walking seemed to be intrinsically connected to Matt.

Even though it was finally starting to sink in that he was alive, she couldn't shake the sensation that something was different. He had barely looked at her since beginning his story, and when he did, it was as though he couldn't bear to meet her eye.

Is he mad at me? Does he blame me for leaving him behind?

She desperately hoped that wasn't true and told herself that wouldn't be like him. More likely he was just in shock—she knew she certainly was.

"You'll come back with us, right?" Joe asked. He glanced around the small room, littered with empty cans and other garbage. The torn mattress had no sheet and was covered in stains. There was a hole in the wall beside a crude drawing of a zombie woman with three breasts. Joe sucked in his breath. "I mean, not that this place isn't great."

Matt laughed. "I don't live here. We found it today. We actually only came into town a few days ago; we've been moving around a lot recently."

"We?" Violet asked.

"Anna and I."

"She's still alive?" Joe sounded surprised. "When you told the story and she wasn't here, I assumed..."

"She's alive, just sleeping next door. I'm surprised she hasn't woken up. I'll just—"

But as Matt spoke, there was movement from the next room, and Anna, tall, beautiful, and barely even ruffled from her sleep, appeared in the doorway. Violet was taken aback by how perfect she was, with smooth hair, flawless skin, and ruby red lips. Anna arched an eyebrow. "Matt?"

"It's alright," he said, getting to his feet. "These are my friends, Joe and Violet."

Anna's eyes flicked between the pair of them, settling on Violet for the longest. She may have been surprised, but her expression remained composed. "Wow, I can't be-lieve it. It appears you're not dead after all."

"Not quite," Joe said, smiling.

"Where do you guys live?" Matt asked. "Where's Toby?"

"We're in a community," Joe explained. "It's called Har-mony. It has walls, lots of people, it's armed, and it's safe."

"Sounds too good to be true," Anna said skeptically.

Joe shook his head. "It's hard work; you have to earn your keep. But it *is* safe."

Matt seemed enthusiastic. "Harmony sounds perfect. What do you think?" He turned to Anna for approval.

She thought for a moment, then wrapped her arm around Matt's waist. "If you think it's a good idea, then I'm with you. Always." She planted a kiss on his lips, then faced Joe and Violet with a smile.

"When shall we leave?"

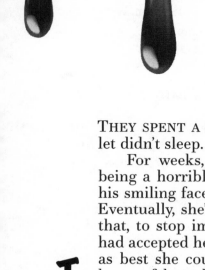

THEY SPENT A FEW HOURS AT THE HOUSE, BUT VIO-
let didn't sleep.

For weeks, she'd fantasized about Matt's death
being a horrible dream, that she'd wake up and see
his smiling face again. But that had never happened.
Eventually, she'd forced herself to stop thinking like
that, to stop imagining a future with him in it. She
had accepted he was dead and moved on with her life
as best she could. Now, she felt guilty. While she'd
been safely tucked in Harmony each night, he'd been
holing up in abandoned buildings, scavenging food,
and judging by his appearance, barely scraping by.
She'd had Joe, Toby, even Ben. Matt had been alone.

Scratch that, not alone. He'd had Anna.

Violet didn't know how to feel about Anna. Something about her didn't sit well.

Could it be the fact that she's flawlessly beautiful,
doesn't trip over her own feet, and probably isn't a
half-zombie?

That might've had something to do with it. Anna
and Matt were clearly an item, if not by the kiss, then
by the way they were curled up together at the other
side of the room. Violet wasn't sure why that made her
feel so uneasy. She and Matt had never been together.
She never even had time to think about whether she
cared for him in that way. They'd been far too busy

87

running from the dead or trying to stop her from eating anyone to have had time for that. It wasn't like she could expect him to harbor feelings for her after thinking she was dead for nine months. It made sense he'd find someone else.

She and Matt were just friends. That was all they'd ever been, and it was all they ever could be. Still, 'just friends' or not, seeing him so close to another girl gave their reunion a slightly bitter taste.

IT TOOK A COUPLE OF HOURS TO WALK BACK TO HARMOny the following morning. They set off while it was still dark, and the sky was just beginning to brighten when they arrived at the gates. Violet had been walking slightly ahead of the other three, but she stopped now, looking up at the watchtower.

"Stay still," she instructed the group.

"Why?" Anna asked, raising her knife and taking hold of Matt's hand in an action that made Violet's skin prickle.

"They'll be pointing their guns at us right now," Joe muttered. "There's always at least two of them watching the road."

On cue, one of the large gates swung open and a figure stepped out. It was Jack. He ran over, pulling Violet into a hug.

After what could only have been a few seconds, but which felt a lot longer, he let go. "When you didn't come back..." he trailed off, still holding onto her shoulders.

Violet interrupted before he could say any more. "We're fine."

He smiled, keeping one arm around her and turning to Joe. "Good to see you." He paused, taking in his bloodied, muddied clothes and bruised face. "You look like crap."

"Ever the charmer," Joe said with a grin. "We brought guests."

Jack eyed Matt and Anna. "That's great. Welcome." He shook their hands in turn, though he'd yet to let go of Violet with his other arm. "Come on, let's get inside."

The sun was now fully up, so Jack gave Matt and Anna a tour of Harmony. Violet and Joe tagged along, too, neither of them willing to leave Matt's side for even a second. He and Anna were polite about the community, asking questions about the people living there and the fortifications. Violet had only ever asked two questions: *"Where do I sleep?"* and *"Does it always smell like that here?"*

The answers had been *"Over there"* and *"Yes."*

They ended the tour by one of the smaller shacks, on the east side of Harmony, near the wall. It was for low point-holders, consisted of one room, and looked to be only moments away from falling down.

"So, this is where you guys can live," Jack began, speaking with an apologetic tone. "I'm sorry, I know it's not much, but you haven't earned any points yet, so..."

Anna smiled. "It's fine. We're happy to be somewhere safe." She regarded Matt affectionately before turning to the others. "We've spent so long running, being in a place surrounded by walls is like a dream." As she spoke, the shack's door handle fell off.

"Oh yeah, a real dream," Matt agreed, clearly stifling a smile.

"Or you could stay with us?" Joe suggested.

Jack shifted a little, his eyes on the floor. That wasn't how it worked. In Harmony, people had to live according to their points.

"I think we'll be okay," Anna said quickly. "We wouldn't want to crowd you, and it's just been the two of us for a long time."

Jack smiled. Violet knew he didn't want to have to argue with them over Ezra's rules, but he had to do his job.

"Hey," Matt called out in surprise as Ben appeared, hopping around his legs and wagging his tail excitedly. Matt knelt, gently stroking his fur. "How have you been, buddy?"

"Matt?"

An expression of delight spread over Matt's face at the sound of Toby's voice. He got to his feet, half stumbling as he hurried over to pick him up and hug him tightly. Toby was talking so quickly that Violet could only make out one word in five.

"Wanted to... couldn't... thought... tried..."

Matt held onto the back of his head, comforting him with quiet words. Toby reached out one hand, pulling Violet in toward the pair. Matt grabbed hold of Joe, and now the four of them were back together, clutching onto each other for the longest time.

THAT MORNING, WHILE MATT AND ANNA SETTLED IN, Violet, Joe, and Toby went back home and found themselves sitting in Violet's room. They were silent at first, the only sound coming from Ben's gentle snores as he slept on her bed. Finally, Joe spoke.

"So... Matt's not dead."

"No," Violet murmured. "I guess not."

"I can't believe it," Toby said quietly. "I thought... I mean, we saw it, didn't we?"

Joe held out his hands. "It was a fake-out death. No one could've predicted that." He smiled. "This is great, though, right?"

Violet nodded.

"So why does it feel weird?" he asked quietly.

"We were sure," Toby muttered. "It doesn't feel real."

"It's been so long," Violet added.

"Who's the woman with him?" Toby asked.

"Anna," Violet replied. "Her name is Anna."

"He met her after we got separated. She was one of the people who saved him," Joe said.

Violet's voice was low. "She's his girlfriend."

Toby sounded confused. "But I thought Vi—"

Joe coughed loudly, cutting him off. Violet shook her head. "We never... Anyway, it doesn't matter now. What matters is that he's alive."

"HOW MUCH FOR THIS?" VIOLET ASKED, HOLDING UP A T-shirt. It was the following morning, and she was in the market, trading points for a couple of essential items. Most of her clothes were torn or covered in blood stains she just couldn't get rid of no matter how long she scrubbed them. She'd spotted the red shirt that morning and thought it might at least hide the inevitable spatters.

"Six points," said the old woman who ran the stall.

The woman had to be at least a hundred and forty, but fought tooth and nail for every point she could get. Violet didn't like trading with her. Not only was she impossible to barter with, but she also had a glass eye that must've been a size too small and tended to drop out mid-conversation. It was more than a little disconcerting. But the old woman somehow always wound up with the best stuff, and Violet had little choice if she wanted to buy something of decent quality.

"Six?" That was a lot for a shirt.

The old woman nodded, her eye wobbling precariously up and down as she did so. "No tears, no holes. Nel's scavengers found it in a fancy store. It's well made."

Violet bit her lip. It wasn't like she didn't have the points, but it was a lot to ask. "Can I try it on?"

"Sure, if you want to strip off right here. I'm afraid our dressing rooms are being refurbished for the summer," the woman replied sarcastically.

Violet scowled. *I'm going to think of a clever and hurtful nickname for you.*

"Hey."

Violet turned and found Matt standing just behind her, smiling awkwardly.

"Hi," she replied, her face flushing to match the color of her shirt. For no reason at all, she felt self-conscious of everything, from the fact that her hair was a mess— tied hurriedly at the top of her head—to the way she was standing. She'd never been like this around Matt before, so why did she feel so uncomfortable now?

Don't say anything stupid.

Just try to act normal.

"You look great," she said enthusiastically, punching his arm and grinning.

Well done. That wasn't weird at all.

But he *did* look great. His clothes had been washed, and he'd had a decent meal. The bags under his eyes were gone from a day and night's worth of sleep, and his eyes were back to their vibrant green.

Violet tried to undo her embarrassing declaration. "I just mean, you look well."

Matt rescued her from her embarrassment. "No, I know what you meant. Thanks. It's been good to get some sleep. I just need a haircut, and then I'll start to feel normal again."

"I can do it," she suggested, smiling at the memory of the last time she had cut his hair. He grinned, too.

"Yeah... maybe."

She laughed, turning back to the stall. Matt came closer, standing beside her. "You're buying this?" He pointed to the red shirt.

"Who knows?" the old woman muttered, her glass eye now pointing at the ceiling. "Been standing here for fifteen minutes. Absolute time waster." She continued to grumble under her breath, walking to the other end of the long table and beginning to fold other items of clothing.

"It's expensive," Violet explained to Matt. "Six points."

He pulled a shocked expression. "What? Six points? Whoa, that's crazy! *Six?*" When Violet rolled her eyes, he shrugged. "Okay, I have no idea how much six points is."

"Clearly."

"How can I start earning my keep?"

"There are different jobs you can do—cleaning, farming, hunting..."

"What do you do?"

"Joe and I are part of a scavenging group. We go out on supply runs and bring stuff back. Depending on what we find, we earn points."

"Can I join?"

Violet thought for a moment. "I'll have to talk to Jack, but I guess we have a couple of openings."

Nice way to say, 'some of our people got killed recently'.

"Jack is your boss?" Matt asked.

"Something like that. I guess."

"It's complicated?"

She nodded. Ezra was technically the only one in charge, but she supposed Jack ranked higher than she did in the grand scheme of things. Not that he ever acted like it.

Matt seemed to understand. "I thought so."

Violet stroked the material of the shirt one more time. "I've made up my mind," she called down the table. "I'll take it."

The old lady sighed, shuffling back over. "Good, excellent. Do you want a bag?"

"Do you have a bag?"

"No, but I can get one of my assistants to bring you one from the back room."

Don't make me eat you, old woman.

Violet's cheeks flushed, but she smiled politely as the old bat printed her name and points on the clipboard in front of her. Then Violet took the T-shirt and held it up against herself, turning back to Matt. "What do you think?"

He smiled. "It looks great."

For some reason that made her feel a little lighter. She flipped the shirt to see the back.

Oh no.

The words 'Kiss me quick, squeeze me slow' were written on the back in a swirling font, with a pair of lips dotting the *I*.

Why didn't you turn the damn thing over before you bought it?

Matt let out a blast of laughter, then tried to compose himself. "Oh, that's... nice."

Violet shook her head. "I didn't see—"

"The lips are a great touch. They really class it up."

"I don't want—"

But Matt could barely hold back his glee at the monstrosity she was holding.

Violet turned helplessly back to the woman. "I'm sorry, this isn't right."

"No refunds."

"But... I didn't realize it said—"

"No refunds."

"It's not exactly a refund," Matt offered, having finally

composed himself. "Couldn't you just cross her name off your list and take the shirt back?"

The woman narrowed her brows, her expression frosty. "No."

Matt's eyes widened, and he held up his hands in surrender. "Okay." He turned back to Violet. "I've changed my mind. I think it's awesome."

She sighed, balling up her purchase and moving away from the stall, wondering bleakly if Joe would trade her something for the hideous thing. He liked to make people laugh, after all. Matt fell into step beside her as they left the warehouse. For a few minutes, neither spoke, but then he broke the silence.

"I'm still trying to come to terms with this."

"I know."

"Doesn't it feel like a lifetime ago that we were together? All of us, I mean."

No, it feels like yesterday. "Mm-hmm."

"I just can't believe you guys were alive this whole time."

"I know, it's kind of strange we didn't run into you. We're out scavenging every week."

Matt shrugged. "We moved around a lot. We only arrived in town a few days ago. Mostly we stayed far away from places we knew had had a lot of people. And we kept away from other survivors."

"Why?"

"A couple of bad encounters."

They were almost at Violet's door now, and Matt stopped walking. "I feel like I should—"

"Matt!"

The two of them turned. Anna jogged over, a smile on her face. She looked even more beautiful, if that were possible, after a good night's sleep. Her hair was pinned up loosely, and soft tendrils framed her heart-shaped face. Her brown eyes sparkled, and when she smiled, her teeth were—like everything else about her—perfect.

"Hey." She flashed Violet those pearly whites, immediately linking arms with Matt. "What are you guys up to?"

"Just talking about the old days," Matt said.

"Mind if I tag along? I'd love to hear some of your stories. Matt never wanted to talk about them before." She stroked his arm playfully. "This guy is a closed book—was he like that when you were friends?"

"We're *still* friends," Matt corrected.

Anna's smile didn't flicker. "Of course. I just mean it's been a long time, and I was wondering if you were always so..." she groped around for the right word. "Mysterious."

Before he could respond, she leaned in and planted a chaste kiss on his lips. "Don't be sensitive; a little mystery is good. In small doses." She winked at Violet. "So, what do you say? Want to fill me in on all the dirt from his past?"

Violet already had her fingers curled around the door handle, a strange, uncomfortable tightening gripping her chest. "Sorry, I need to go."

"Are you sure?" Anna asked.

"Yes... I need to use the bathroom. I have a stomach-ache." She turned, pushing open the door and half stumbling in her haste to get away.

That's great. What a lovely image to leave them with, you running to the bathroom to presumably have explosive diarrhea.

She leaned against the closed door of the apartment. What was wrong with her?

ELEVEN

"Buses?" Violet raised an eyebrow, not sure she'd heard Jack right. "Ezra wants buses?"

"He thinks they'd be useful for forming barricades when we start expanding the fences. Plus, we'd need them if we ever had to move a lot of people around."

"Why would we have to do that?" Lex asked.

Jack shrugged. "Don't ask me. I just know that he's asked us to find some, so that's what we're going to do."

"How many does he want?"

"At least three, so we're joining up with Nel's group. Carl's, too."

Nel and Carl led the two other scavenging teams, which were both much larger than Jack's. Violet had only seen Carl a couple of times, usually when he was buying alcohol from the markets. He was harmless, she supposed, and good with his group, but he drank a lot and she wondered how much he could be counted on if a swarm of biters descended during a run.

Nel, on the other hand, was pretty intimidating. It wasn't the way she looked—on the surface, she appeared to be just like any other thirty-something-year-old woman. She had blonde hair that was always pulled into a ponytail, and she wore a green, army-style jacket that was a little too big for her. Violet assumed it had once belonged to someone else.

No, Nel was scary in other ways. She was one of Ezra's top lieutenants, and her scavenging group consistently found the best stuff. She carried a machine gun but could do almost as much damage to a person with a single word. She was strong, confident, and not afraid to speak her mind.

Nel was currently doing just that—yelling at two of her men for giving her the wrong car. They looked as though they both wanted the ground to swallow them up. Carl and his people were laughing quietly from their spot not far away. Violet and the others watched as Nel finished her tirade.

"Do you think I should be more like that?" Jack muttered.

Violet couldn't help but smile. He was the most laidback of Ezra's soldiers. "I'm not sure you could pull it off," she replied.

He winked, squeezing her shoulder as Nel, happy that her men had been suitably reprimanded, strode over. Everyone in the vicinity automatically stood up a little straighter.

"Are your people ready?" she asked, eyes sweeping across the group.

Jack nodded. "Just waiting for a couple more."

"Then you're not ready, are you?"

Jack simply smiled, speaking through slightly gritted teeth. "No, I suppose not."

"Hurry up, we're leaving now." Nel took one last look at the four of them, eyes settling on Joe for the longest, and then headed back to her car.

Joe raised an eyebrow. "Do you think she fancies me?"

"I think she was deciding whether or not to kill that thing on your face," Lex muttered.

"Who are we waiting for?" Violet asked Jack, who was glancing over her shoulder.

"Them."

She turned. Matt and Anna were making their way, hand in hand, across the courtyard.

"Morning," Anna said, smiling brightly.

Oh good. This is just what I need, a day with the lovebirds.

Violet forced a smile across her lips as Anna and Matt climbed into the back of the car.

Joe caught her eye. "Are you okay?"

"Yeah, why?"

"Your face looks weird."

"I'm smiling."

He raised an eyebrow. "I'm not sure that's what that is, but alright." He climbed into the backseat next to Matt.

Lex went to get into the front, but Violet pulled her aside. "Can I ride up front today?"

"No." Lex probably wasn't meaning to be rude, but she never minced words. Violet wasn't about to give up that easily.

"Please."

"Why?"

"I just..." she trailed off. She didn't have an answer, not really. It was simply the idea of being crammed into the back of a car with Matt and Anna, still holding hands, made her feel uncomfortable.

Lex shrugged. "Whatever. If it really means that much to you." She joined Joe in the back, whose protests about lack of space were ignored as she climbed onto his lap.

Violet let out a sigh of relief, sliding into the front seat. Jack smiled as she closed the door. "Ready to go?"

Just a simple run. What could go wrong?

FINDING BUSES WASN'T TOO HARD. EZRA, AS USUAL, HAD good information, and he'd given them directions to a depot where the vehicles were stored.

Nel, as the self-appointed leader of all three groups, gathered everyone together. "Get into pairs and check this place is secure."

Joe was with Ryan, Lex chose a girl from Nel's group who carried her axe with the same enthusiasm she did, and Anna and Matt were already holding hands, so Violet paired up with Jack. They walked along the rows of buses in silence. Jack used his flashlight to illuminate their path.

"You need more batteries?" he asked when he realized

she wasn't using hers.

"Yeah."

"Do you not have enough points?"

"I'm running low after I blew six on this shirt." She unzipped her jacket to show him.

"That's nice."

"Oh yeah?" She lowered the jacket at the back and turned around. He shone his light on the writing, and then laughed. "Wow, that's... wow."

"Uh-huh."

She zipped her jacket back up, and they continued on in silence.

"You've been a bit preoccupied recently," Jack began, sounding concerned. "I wasn't sure if anything was wrong?"

Violet had no idea where to start. She couldn't even explain to herself why she felt so weird, let alone to anyone else. Luckily, her awkwardness was cut short as Nel's voice carried across the huge space.

"Talk to me."

"Clear," Jack called, along with several others.

"Then let's get moving."

They headed back to the entrance and found Nel standing in the middle of an open space in front of several buses.

"This is how it's going to work," she began briskly. "We'll take three buses today, then come back for the others." She gestured to the one behind her. "I'll take this one with you, you, and you."

She continued splitting everyone between the vehicles, and Violet, Jack, Matt, Anna, two of Nel's people, and three of Carl's were in the last group. One of Nel's men was charged with driving. Violet thought he was called Dennis, but being legendarily terrible at remembering names, she decided it would be best not to speak to him at all.

After everyone else had climbed on board, she and Jack made to get on at the same time, almost bumping into each other in the process.

"Oh, sorry," Violet mumbled.

"Sorry."

"After you," they both said at the same time, stepping back in unison. They both smiled, then almost bumped into each other as they attempted to get on again. Violet snorted involuntarily.

One day you'll stop being so awkward.

Jack held out his hand, gesturing for her to get in first. She climbed inside, stumbling over her own feet.

Today is not that day.

WHILE NEL'S MAN—WHO VIOLET WAS NOW ALMOST CERtain was called Martin, not Dennis—worked on getting the bus started, she found a seat near the back. A few rows ahead, Anna was laughing at something Matt had said, gently brushing his hair out of his eyes. He grinned, and for some reason this made Violet's stomach sink. Jack dropped into the seat in front of her and leaned over the back, watching her curiously.

"What happened with you two?" he asked, nodding in Matt's direction.

"What do you mean?"

"You know what I mean. Were you together?"

Violet darted a glance at them. Anna was still laughing, her hand resting on Matt's shoulder. "No. We were only ever friends. Just friends."

A smile played on Jack's lips. "Sure."

"What?" For some reason, his response irritated her.

"Nothing."

She sat up straighter. "No, come on. Clearly, you've got something to say, so say it."

Jack widened his eyes. "Wow, calm down." He held his hands up in playful surrender. "I was going to say that the way you were looking at him made me think maybe something had happened between you. Now that you're getting all weird and defensive, I definitely think you had some kind of thing."

Violet's cheeks blazed. "We did not."

Realizing he'd hit a nerve, his tone softened. "Okay, sorry. My mistake."

"I was never *flung*."

Jack bit his lip, and she realized how ridiculous she sounded.

She put her head down on the seat in front of her with a groan. "That's not what it's called."

"No. Not for normal people, anyway." Jack stroked her hair sympathetically as she internally scolded herself for being such an idiot. The bus shuddered to life, and Violet sat back in her seat as they exited the depot into the bright sunshine. The other two vehicles had long gone, but it didn't matter. They knew how to get home, and this was probably one of the safest ways to travel.

Jack was still watching her, not about to let the Matt thing end just yet. "Seriously? Nothing happened with you two? Not even once?"

"No. Never. I've never even had..." Violet cut herself off, aware of what she'd inadvertently said. It was too late to take it back, though, and Jack was unable to hide the surprise from his face.

"Never? Not with anyone?"

"Oh good, this is a conversation I really want to be having." She sighed, the burning in her face returning with a vengeance.

"Don't be embarrassed."

"I'm not embarrassed, not really." To be honest, it wasn't something she'd spent a lot of time thinking about. Losing her virginity hadn't exactly been at the top of Violet's to-do list since the dead had risen. Though she had to admit, it wasn't the greatest title to have when compared to her friends:

Lex: Destroyer of Zombies
Joe: Comedian
Jack: Soldier
Matt: Survivor
Violet: Virgin

"I guess I was waiting for the right person," she said, finally.

"Was that person Matt?"

Violet scowled. Jack was like a dog with a bone. "We were just friends."

"But you wanted it to be more?"

Why won't this conversation just end?

Before she could open her mouth to respond, the bus swerved to the left violently. There were screams. Everyone was thrown out of their seats as the bus skidded along on two wheels. Violet was only aware that she was flying forward for a couple of seconds before everything went dark.

VIOLET WOKE WITH HER HEAD POUNDING. SLOWLY, SHE opened her eyes a fraction, reaching up to wipe at the trickle of blood drying on her temple. She was lying on her side.

Wait, no, the bus is on its side.

She was leaning against the window, which had been partially shattered by a rock, now digging uncomfortably into her shoulder. Gingerly, she sat up, eyes scanning the wreckage for others. There were bodies. Several. She couldn't tell who they were. None of them seemed to be moving. The air was foggy with smoke. Something was on fire, but she couldn't see what it was yet. Nevertheless, it was probably a good idea to get the hell off the bus. She got onto all fours and crawled to the nearest body. It was one of Carl's men. He had a head wound, but Violet knew he was dead because his blood didn't make her head spin. At least not any more than it already was. She needed to get out of there quickly—if anyone were still alive but bleeding, she could lose control.

Clambering over windows and the sides of seats, she made her way to the emergency exit at the back, holding her breath and avoiding getting too close to the other bodies. She had no idea how long the bus had been on its side, but it was getting dark. It had to be sheer dumb luck that the biters hadn't found the wreckage. How much longer would that last?

Something grabbed her ankle, and Violet cried out, kicking back against the hand. It let go, and she heard a familiar voice.

"It's me," Jack groaned. "Please don't make that noise again—my head is barely holding together as it is." There was a lot of blood on his face, but though it was making her a little dizzy, it was dry enough that she felt relatively safe being so close.

"I feel like crap," he murmured, reaching up to touch his head.

"I think you'll live," she replied, trying not to breathe too deeply as she pulled him into a sitting position. "Come on, let's get off this thing." But suddenly she realized he could help her. She had no idea where Matt was and couldn't risk getting too close in case he was bleeding. But Jack could.

"Can you check and see if Matt is still on the bus?" she asked.

Jack didn't ask why she wasn't coming, too; he simply turned and began to crawl to the front of the bus. She forced open the emergency exit and fell as gracefully as ever onto the road.

There was a chill in the air, and the last few streaks of sunlight were disappearing over the horizon. Wherever the other buses were, they hadn't come back to help. Violet's jacket was ripped, but she kept it on, shivering as the wind whipped across her face. She stood still for a moment, trying to formulate a plan while she waited for Jack. It was better than thinking about whether Matt had survived the crash. Regardless of how many survivors there were, a choice had to be made quickly. They could try to get back to Harmony tonight, on foot and still weak from the accident, or they could spend the night outside the walls.

They appeared to have tipped over on an empty road in the middle of a wooded area. Thick trees surrounded the road on both sides, which probably accounted for the lack of biters.

As the wind rustled the trees once more, Violet heard another sound—feet on tarmac. Something was coming.

"Jack, hurry up," she hissed into the open door. She didn't have a weapon—her third crowbar was still on the bus somewhere.

"Violet?" Matt came around the side of the bus, bruised and bloodied, but alive. For some reason, he was only wearing one shoe. He didn't get too close, presumably because of the blood, but she could smell that it was safe enough.

"I'm so glad you're okay," Violet said. She lowered her voice and added, "Don't worry about the blood. It's dry."

Matt relaxed. "That's good."

"Is it just you out here?" she asked.

As if on cue, Anna appeared, slipping her knife into her belt. "We're clear. No shufflers except the ones the bus hit," she muttered. She gave Violet a quick smile.

Violet returned it, then pointed at the bus. "Jack is in there. I don't know if anyone else made it."

At that moment, Jack's head poked out of the back doors. He struggled to meet Violet's gaze, his voice low. "Vi, I'm so sorry. I think he's—" He paused, catching sight of Matt. "Oh, hi. Glad you're okay." He climbed out of the bus, holding up a sneaker in one hand and tossing it to him. "Found your shoe."

"Thanks." Matt quirked an eyebrow. "Were you about to say I was dead?"

Jack shrugged. "I found your shoe."

"So you immediately assumed I had died?"

"I don't know. It was just weird. What living person leaves one shoe behind?"

Matt looked bemused. "But the alternative is that my shoe came off, and I, what? Disintegrated into the floor? Did you work for the police before all this?"

There was a crunch of feet over broken glass, and all four of them turned to face different directions.

"Jack, were there any other survivors?" Violet asked.

He shook his head.

"Are you as sure as you were that I was dead," Matt asked, "or did you just count shoes?"

"We need to leave," Anna interrupted. "It's a miracle the dead haven't found us already." She jerked her head to the left, in the direction the bus had been traveling. "There's a sign over there. It says there's a town up ahead." Pulling her knife back out, she began jogging in that di-

rection. The others followed.

T
W
E
L
V
E

THEY FOUND AN OLD OFFICE BUILDING ON THE OUT-skirts of town, which seemed a safe enough place to seek shelter for the night. Walking back to Harmony in the dark, with only one flashlight and no idea how long the journey would take, it probably wasn't the smartest idea. Jack had grabbed their weapons from the bus, though, so at least they weren't totally un-protected.

The building had clearly housed survivors before. In the largest room on the second floor, six desks had been pushed neatly against the wall, while three blan-kets and a large pan containing the charred remains from several fires took precedence in the center of the room.

Whoever had owned those things was obviously long gone. It didn't look like anyone had slept in the blankets or cooked anything in the pan for at least a couple of weeks. Jack secured the door by moving some desks in front of it, and Anna began searching through a stack of food cans to see if any were un-opened.

"Why do you think the other buses didn't come back?" Matt asked Violet, joining her by the window.

"I don't know," she answered truthfully. "Even if they thought we were dead, Joe and Lex would've wanted to check. I hope nothing happened to them."

"I'm sure they're fine."

She watched as Jack moved over to the pan and set to work starting a fire inside it.

"He seems like a good guy," Matt said.

"Yeah."

"I mean, he thought I was dead because I lost a shoe, but other than that."

Violet smiled, and he continued. "He takes care of you?"

"Yeah, I guess he does." There was movement just below the window, and she stepped back, drawing the blinds. If they were going to get a fire going, she didn't want the dead to see the light.

"How are you?" Matt asked. "That crash was pretty intense."

"I'm fine, just a bit of a headache. Did you see how it happened?"

He shook his head. "No, but Anna said we hit some biters. Enough of those could make the bus swerve and tip over. I guess we did enough damage to the dead to stop them getting up again, though, which is lucky." He took a step closer, lowering his voice. "You were passed out when I woke up, but Anna was still bleeding, so I took her outside to clean her up. I didn't want you to..." He trailed off.

"Thanks."

He squeezed her arm, and then the room was bathed in a dim orange glow.

"Success," Jack called triumphantly, holding up both arms. Anna smiled, gesturing for Matt to come and sit beside her on one of the blankets. He gave Violet's arm a final squeeze, then headed over. She followed, taking another blanket to herself. Jack dropped down on the third. For a while, they sat in a circle around the fire, saying nothing but enjoying the warmth. Violet wriggled out of her torn jacket.

"Cool shirt," Anna said. "Love the color."

"Get her to show you the best bit," Matt teased.

Violet rolled her eyes, turning around to share the hideous message on the back.

Anna grinned. "That's nice."

"Awful, right?" Violet muttered. "I hate it."

"Wanna trade?" Anna asked. "I'll wear it." She got to her feet without waiting for a reply, taking her own T-shirt off and holding it out.

Why is she not wearing a bra? Literally thousands of ransacked stores, ripe for looting, and she can't pick up a single piece of underwear?

Jack's mouth hung open, while Matt focused on his shoes.

Violet shook her head. "It's... I'm fine... thanks."

Anna casually pulled her shirt back on and sat back down beside Matt. "No problem."

Now let's all sit here and pretend you didn't just get your breasts out.

"What's your favorite food?" Jack asked out of nowhere.

"What?"

He shrugged. "I was just thinking about how good it would be to have something to eat. What would you have if you could have anything?"

Anna answered immediately. "Fried chicken—the greasier the better."

"Really?" Jack raised an eyebrow, eyeing Anna's slender figure. "I never would've guessed that."

"It was always my weakness."

"Mine would be cheeseburgers," he said. "With extra bacon." He looked over to Violet for her answer. She struggled to remember what she had enjoyed before food lost all flavor. After an awkwardly long amount of time, she lamely answered, "Chocolate."

"Good choice," Anna said. "Matt?"

He thought for a moment. "Back when we were all in the school, Violet used to make this weird pasta thing."

"Sounds delicious," Jack said, grinning wickedly.

Matt laughed. "I can't really explain it, but it was really good. Before that I'd pretty much just been eating chips and candy, so it was the first real meal I'd eaten after everything went to hell. I guess that's probably why it's my favorite."

Violet felt a warmth spreading through her that was only partially caused by the fire.

"I've got one," Anna said. "What's the best part of the zompocalypse?"

"Wow, so many things to choose from," Jack mused.

Matt stroked his chin thoughtfully. "I know—running for your life, flesh eating corpses, sleeping in abandoned buildings on dirty old blankets..."

Anna pushed him playfully. "Come on, just play the game. For me, it's no more crowds."

"I like the quiet," Jack agreed. "It's nice not to have all that noise anymore."

"Besides all the screaming, you mean?" Violet countered.

He smiled. "Yeah, besides that. Plus, I was kind of a loner before, and now I'm part of something. That's a good thing."

"Not having to worry about money is pretty cool," Matt said. "I was always worried I wouldn't be able to buy a house and get a mortgage, but now I don't need to. I can just live anywhere I want... as long as it's, you know, abandoned. And not full of zombies."

"I wouldn't have met most of my best friends if it wasn't for this," Violet chipped in. "I suppose that's the best part."

"What would be your biggest wish?" Jack asked, leaning back. "If you could have anything you want, right now."

"For things to go back to normal," Anna answered.

"I thought you said you liked the lack of crowds?" Matt asked.

She raised an eyebrow. "I'd take a crowd to get rid of the flesh-eating corpses. And to get my phone back. I miss my phone."

"I just want to be able to keep my friends safe," Jack said. "I don't know if I could go back to everything being *normal* after all this, but being able to keep everyone alive... that would be what I'd wish for."

They waited for Matt's answer, but he didn't appear to have one. His expression suggested he was somewhere far away. Moments later, his attention was brought back to the room. "I don't know... no more zombies, I guess." He didn't sound entirely sincere, but no one probed him further. Violet couldn't help but feel like the mood in the room had shifted. Jack, however, was ready with the next question, his attention on Anna.

"Okay, what about your biggest fear?"

She bit her lip, speaking quietly. "Being alone. The worst time of my life was when I was alone. I don't think I could go through that again." She reached for Matt's hand and squeezed it.

Jack nodded. "Mine is not being as strong as my brother."

"I didn't know you had a brother," Violet said. He'd never mentioned one before.

"He died just before I met you." He lowered his head, and she stretched out to touch his arm.

"I'm sorry."

He gave a small nod, then looked over at Matt. "What about you? What's your biggest fear?"

"Well... you know... the zombies."

Jack laughed, and Violet couldn't help but smile.

"What about you, Vi?"

All eyes were on her, but just as she was about to make a joke, Anna snuggled closer to Matt, resting her head on his shoulder. She took one of his hands in her own and placed it on her leg. She was relaxed, so comfortable, so at ease, and suddenly it was as though all the oxygen had been wrenched out of Violet's lungs.

"Are you okay?" Jack asked, sounding worried.

She nodded, her mouth dry. Her joke answer fell right out of her head, and she stumbled to her feet. "I'm just going to get some air." Before anyone could ask anything else, she hurried to the window, forcing it open and hanging her head outside. The cool night air felt good after the heat of the fire, and she took deep lungfuls, trying to clear her foggy thoughts.

What's wrong with you?

But she didn't want to think about that question too deeply, because whether she liked it or not, she knew exactly what had made her feel so sick.

WHEN VIOLET WOKE UP THE FOLLOWING MORNING, SUN-light was shining weakly through the dusty windows. It was early. She stretched, her joints popping from a night on the thin blanket. Everyone else was still sleeping soundly. Anna was even more beautiful when she was asleep, if that were even possible, and Violet tried not to hate her for it.

You can't hate someone for being beautiful; that's ridiculous.

It *was* ridiculous, totally ridiculous. But as Violet got up and walked past the pair of them, she had a flighting desire to chop off Anna's beautiful brown locks and see if she was still quite so pretty with a shaved head.

She sighed. It wasn't Anna's fault she was flawless while Violet herself often looked as though she'd been dragged through a hedge. Backward. In the rain. By a bear.

She decided to go and find a bathroom, carefully unblocking the door and stepping out into the silent hallway. No sign of the dead at least. She spotted the bathroom just past the stairs leading down to the entrance and padded toward it.

It was basic, but clean, with a large tin bath in the corner of the room. Violet supposed the previous residents had bathed and washed their clothes there. Walking to the row of sinks along the wall, she decided to risk a glance in the mirror.

Zompocalypse-chic was not Violet's look. Her hair had, as usual, mostly worked loose from her braid. It hung in tangles and smelled more than a little of mildew, thanks to a night on the old blanket. She had dark circles under her gray eyes, and though she was used to her skin being incredibly pale due to infection, this morning she looked even more like a walking corpse. And that was only half true.

She ran the tap on the off chance and was surprised to find water still in the tank. She splashed a little on her face.

Wow, that made all the difference. You're a vision.

She scowled, trying to ignore the insults from the voice in her head as she pulled the rest of her hair free from the braid and dunked it under the water. It was cold, and she didn't have any shampoo, but at least it would get rid of the smell from those hideous blankets. She wrung it out, ran her fingers through the tangles, and pulled it back into a braid again. Still not perfect, but better at least.

She headed out of the bathroom, planning to go back and tell the others about the running water. Footsteps on the stairs to her right forced her to stop.

Well, crap.

Six biters were ascending the stairs toward her. Violet charged back down the hall, barreling into the room and slamming the door shut. The noise woke the others. Jack and Anna sat bolt upright, but Matt stayed horizontal and put one hand on his head, sighing.

"Zombies?"

His question was answered by hands pounding on the door. Jack hurried to help move the desk back in place.

Matt got to his feet. "I guess it's time to leave." He moved to the window, opening it as wide as it could go. "There's a roof about four feet down. We can climb out."

"Good," Anna muttered, making to exit first. "I've had enough of this place anyway."

THIRTEEN

THEY MADE IT BACK TO HARMONY JUST AS THE GATES were swinging open, and Violet saw Joe, Lex, Toby, and Ryan heading out. Joe was yelling something angrily over his shoulder. He stopped in his tracks when he caught sight of Violet and the others, a huge grin spreading slowly across his face as he jogged toward them and threw his arms around her neck.

"You have no idea how happy I am to see you," he said, eventually letting her go.

"What happened?" Lex asked, looking more worried about them than Violet would've ever given her credit for. "When the bus didn't show up—"

"We wanted to go back and search for you," Joe interrupted, "but Nel said if her man didn't make it back, then no one could have. She didn't even want to send anyone to check."

"So, you were coming out alone?" Violet asked. That was completely against the rules—they were always supposed to have one of Ezra's soldiers when they left.

Lex nodded. "They weren't willing to go with us, so we said we'd do it by ourselves."

"They weren't happy about it," Toby said. "Especially after what Joe called them."

"And their moms," Lex added.

"Yeah, yeah, that doesn't matter now," Joe said

hurriedly. "Let's just get back inside."

"So you can apologize?" Lex guessed.

"Apologize, grovel, offer to clean their boots... whatever it takes to make sure they don't shoot me."

THE NEXT MORNING, EVERYONE WAS CALLED TO EZRA'S stage. Their leader had an announcement to make. As soon as Violet saw him, she felt nervous. By the way he was pacing, it was clear something was wrong. Everyone else seemed to sense it, too, and as the crowd gathered, the air thickened with tension.

"Friends," Ezra began after a long silence. "I've gathered you all here because I have some unfortunate news. Someone among us is a traitor."

The crowd was silent. Violet, like every other person, kept her eyes fixed on Ezra. Her mind, however, was buzzing. What did he mean 'traitor'? What earned a person that title in Harmony? In all the time she had been there, life had been relatively peaceful. Sure, there was the odd fight or incident of theft, but those were dealt with swiftly by the soldiers, and people rarely committed a crime twice. Harmony didn't have a jail, and they certainly didn't execute anyone, so the punishment for criminal activity was simple. One crime, such as violence or stealing, could be paid for through community service, the length of which was decided based on the severity of the offense. But anyone who broke the rules twice was banished. Their family, if they had one, was offered the choice to stay or leave. Most chose to stay, despite knowing it meant they would never see their loved one again. Everyone in Harmony had come from the world outside, and they were in no hurry to go back to it.

More serious crimes, like murder, just didn't occur. Not within the walls.

Ezra continued. "Someone—whose identity remains a mystery for now—snuck into my home and took something that belongs to me."

A sharp intake of breath from the crowd. No one stole

from Ezra. Not only would the fear of being caught by the soldiers be enough to dissuade anyone, but people respected the man. He'd built the very community that kept them safe.

Who would be that stupid?

Ezra allowed a moment for his words to sink in, then began pacing the stage once more. "Two of my vassals are missing. They would not, and could not, have left this place without help." He paused, surveying everyone slowly. "Know this: I do not take kindly to thieves."

With that he left, heading back to his home above the warehouse.

"I don't understand," Matt asked as he and Anna joined Violet and Jack. "What's he talking about?"

"His vassals, the ones who work in his place," Jack explained. "They live in the warehouse and get the best food, best clothes, and answer directly to Ezra. They never have to go outside of Harmony."

"What did he mean when he said they'd been stolen? They're people, right?"

"Makes them sound like slaves," Anna added.

Violet shook her head. "We're all free to go if we want. No one has to stay here."

"Have you ever seen it, though?" Joe asked, joining them. "Anyone leaving?"

She thought for a moment, then shook her head. She'd never seen anyone leave Harmony, but that was hardly surprising. Here they were safe, protected by soldiers and the wall. They had food and supplies. Outside there was nothing but running, hunger, and death.

"I just don't get why the vassals would *want* to go," Jack muttered, lowering his voice as a couple of other soldiers passed. "They had the best deal, right?"

"Being a slave sounds super fun," Anna said sarcastically.

"They're not slaves," Violet insisted. "They get paid."

"Whatever." Anna waved her hand, eyes flicking to the empty stage. "That guy is creepy. Does he usually talk like that? It was like he was threatening all of us."

"It's not normally like this," Violet said. But deep down,

she wasn't sure if that was true. Maybe she'd just never noticed it before.

⎍〜⏜⋀⋀⋀⋀⏜⎍＿＿＿＿＿＿＿＿＿＿

"YOU DON'T HAVE TO COME, YOU KNOW," JOE SAID. HE WAS sitting on his bed, watching as Violet put her shoes on. It had been half an hour since Ezra's announcement, and now they had a job to do. "You can take a day."

Violet raised an eyebrow. "I spent one night outside the walls. I'm fine. We were out there together when we found Matt, and you weren't worried about me then."

Joe shrugged. "I was with you. Besides, I was thinking more about the horrific bus crash than you having to spend a night on a moldy blanket."

"Oh yeah." She had practically forgotten about the bus. "I'm fine. I want to do this." It was true. She had been feeling a little strange since Ezra's speech and thought getting out of Harmony for a few hours might help.

A couple of Ezra's people had spotted some chickens wandering around a farm not too far away, but they'd been unable to collect them. Jack's scavenging group was tapped to go and catch as many as they could. Over the past few months, they'd built up a sizable collection of farm animals, which they kept just outside the walls and had armed guards watch over them at all times. They had no chickens yet, though, and eggs would be a valuable addition to their food supply.

The scavenging group travelled out of town, eventually reaching a long dirt driveway that led to the farm where the birds had last been spotted. As they got closer, Violet saw the blue farmhouse wasn't holding up too well. Several windows were broken, and the roof had collapsed on one side. The front door hung on a slant, as though it might fall off its hinges at any moment.

"Any sign of the chickens?" Jack asked once everyone was gathered outside.

Matt pointed to the ground just ahead of him. "There are scratch marks around here, fairly recent. They can't be far."

Jack examined the ground, then nodded. "Good find. Let's split up."

They took off in pairs, Violet and Joe walking together.

"Since when did Matt become the chicken whisperer?" Joe asked.

She smiled.

"Are you okay?" He still sounded worried.

"Stop asking me that; I'm fine. The bus only crashed a little bit."

Joe grinned. "Well that's good, but I didn't mean just that."

"I don't understand."

"It's just that... ever since Matt—"

"There," Violet cut him off, pointing at a flock of at least twenty chickens of varying sizes and colors scratching around in the dirt ahead of them. Lex and Toby were already there. As Violet and Joe approached, Jack appeared, driving one of the cars and parking around ten feet away from the nearest bird. He got out, closed his door quietly, and began to grab cardboard and plastic boxes from the backseat and the trunk.

"Okay," Jack began as the others regrouped. "The plan is to get the birds into the boxes as quickly as possible."

Joe raised an eyebrow. "That's it?"

"What?"

"I don't know. The way you gathered us here, I thought you needed to explain something really complex. Not 'just shove the things into the boxes before they fly away'."

"That's wrong," Lex said. "Chickens don't fly."

Joe's face was deadpan. "They're birds."

"So are penguins," Violet cut in. "They don't fly, either. Lex is right."

Joe shook his head. "No, she's never right."

"*Anyway*," Jack interrupted, "the point is, we need to be fast. We don't want the rest of the birds to... escape. Flying or not."

Within five minutes, the group was chasing chickens around the yard. They'd managed to corner the feathery beasts relatively quickly, but the job still wasn't easy.

Lex stood up straight beside Violet, rubbing the base of her spine. Her dark hair was already clinging to her face thanks to her exertion and the hot sun. "Remind me why we're doing this again?"

"We're doing our bit for the community?" Violet suggested.

"That doesn't sound right."

"We like animals?"

"You do. I don't."

"We want to eat chicken nuggets?"

Lex grinned. "That's more like it." She made to grab the next bird with increased vigor, caught it, and shoved it unceremoniously into the box at her feet. "Next!"

"How about this," Joe called from his spot not far away. "What do you call a sleeping cow?"

Lex said nothing, giving Violet a weary look.

"Go on," Violet called back. "What do you call a sleeping cow?"

"A bulldozer!"

"Joe, that's just awful."

He came over, his arms shredded from his attempts to capture the birds. "Try this," he continued, unfazed. "What do you call a cow with a twitch?"

"What?"

"Beef jerky."

Lex scowled. "Don't you have anywhere else to be irritating?"

"Not until five." He grinned widely. "What do you call a cow that doesn't give milk?"

"I don't want—"

"A milk dud!"

Violet shook her head. "I feel like these are getting worse."

"Why are they all about cows?" Lex asked.

"I don't have any vegetable jokes yet, so if you do, lettuce know."

Violet snorted. "That was pretty good."

"Is it just me, or are farm jokes corny?" Jack laughed at his own pun as he approached.

Lex rolled her eyes. "Jesus, there's two of them." She

moved away toward another group of birds.

Joe winked at Violet and followed Lex, clearly planning to grace her with more of his A-grade comedy.

Jack leaned against the fence, his eyes focused over Violet's shoulder. She followed his gaze, watching as Matt and Anna tried to catch one bird with a limp, who was still managing to avoid every attempt they made. They were both laughing.

"They seem to have settled in," Jack said.

"Yeah."

"Do you trust him?"

"What?" That was a strange question. "You think I shouldn't?"

"I didn't say that."

"Do *you* trust him?"

"I never trust a survivor until I know what they did to last this long."

Violet thought of Matt, out there without walls to protect him. She thought of the kinds of people she and Joe had come across, the dangerous situations they'd found themselves in during simple scavenging runs. They had been attacked countless times, often barely managing to escape with their lives. Matt hadn't had somewhere safe to go at night; his life had been in constant danger. What things might he have done just to survive?

"Look at this cock!"

Violet turned at Joe's voice, immensely relieved to see him holding a cockerel at arm's length. It was fighting to break free, scratching his arms to pieces, but he still held it triumphantly.

"I can't tell you how relieved I am that he was talking about a bird," Jack murmured.

But Violet couldn't get her mind off Jack's question. Her eyes flicked to Matt. He certainly looked different, almost haunted—as though he'd been through more than she could understand. She wasn't scared of him, she doubted that was possible. Did she still trust him, though?

"Sonofa—" Joe cried out in exasperation as the bird in his arms struggled free of his grasp, flapping its wings wildly and landing in the dust a few feet away. It gave Joe one last glance, as if plotting vengeance, before running in the other direction. Strangely, though, this made Joe whoop in vindication, and he turned to Lex victoriously. "Told you!"

She raised an eyebrow. "Told me what?"

"The cockerel! It flew!"

"That wasn't flight."

"It flapped its wings and moved through the air. What would *you* call that?"

Lex shrugged. "You'd flap your arms if I pushed you out of a window. It still wouldn't be flying."

"I wouldn't go as far as that bird just did."

"Shall we try it?"

Jack interrupted their debate as he stepped closer to the pair and pointed at the farmhouse, squinting against the bright sunlight. "You see that?"

Violet followed his gaze. Yes, she saw it—movement from the upstairs window. "Biters?" she asked.

"Not sure. But there's something up there." He whistled, catching the attention of the others, and motioned for them to follow him to the back door of the house. It was unlocked and opened with a squeak, allowing them into the kitchen. The place had clearly been inhabited for the past few days—the coating of dust on most surfaces had been roughly swept clear on several chairs as well as the counter where food had recently been prepared. The windows were covered with sheets nailed haphazardly to the tops of the warped wooden frames. There were some children's drawings stuck on the fridge, the paper curled and faded, but Violet didn't look at them.

Jack led the group to the staircase, where footprints in the dust signaled the recent movement of people, and headed up first. The others followed, except for Ryan and Toby, who stayed behind to keep watch at the door.

It was relatively bright upstairs. Though dirty, the windows were uncovered, allowing the sunlight to stream through. All the doors in the hallway were open except for the last one on the left. If she had to guess, Violet would put money on there being people hiding in that room. Jack went there first and tried the handle. The door opened slowly. It was a large bedroom, which appeared, at first glance, to be clear of both living and dead inhabitants. There was a double bed, a dressing table, and two big armoires. For a moment, none of the group seemed to know what to do. Then Violet saw Jack's eyes settle on the bed.

He thinks they're under it.

He motioned to the others to have their weapons ready, then held up his fingers.

Three, two, one.

Jack, Joe, and Matt reached under the bed. There were brief sounds of a struggle before a man and woman were roughly yanked out from underneath. They were both young, incredibly skinny, and had the same curly red hair and bright blue eyes. Violet wondered if they were brother and sister.

"Okay, okay!" the man said, no longer fighting. He held his hands up in surrender. "Please, we don't want no trouble. That's why we hid."

Jack and Matt released their grip on him, and Joe let go of the woman. Violet noticed she was missing a couple of teeth. The woman's ivory skin was dirty, and her hair was tangled and matted. The man was covered in a layer of grime as well, though he at least had all of his teeth.

"We got no weapons," he continued. "Lost my knife yesterday."

The woman held up her own filthy hands to show they, too, were empty.

"We came for the chickens," Jack said, quirking his head to the window.

"We thought so. That's fine, take 'em. Just don't hurt us."

"Why would we hurt you?" Anna asked. Violet wondered if she meant to sound quite so irritated. She was certainly observing the pair as though they were something unpleasant that had crawled out of a drain.

The woman shrugged, hands still slightly raised. "That's what everyone does now, right?"

The man ran a hand through his hair. "We lost six of our friends. They were taken by people—living people, just like you."

"Who?" Violet asked.

"Don't know who they are, only that they came in a truck and dragged most of us away. We hid; they didn't know we were here, but they took our friends." His face dropped.

Violet tried to imagine what it would be like to make that choice, to hide to save yourself while your friends were dragged off by strangers.

The man sniffed. "They were talking about impressing some guy. Guess he's their leader."

"Ezra," the woman muttered. "They said, 'Another six for Ezra.'"

"Ezra?" Violet's head spun. She looked at her friends, but they appeared to be just as confused as she was. "That can't be right. Are you sure they said Ezra?"

The pair threw worried glances at each other. "You're one of them?" the man asked.

"We don't *take* anyone," Jack insisted. "We offer a safe place, but only if they want to join. We don't drag people into trucks."

But the man and woman were holding up their hands again.

"Please, please just let us go." The man's voice cracked as he spoke.

"This is just a misunderstanding," Violet said, shaking her head. "It's a mistake."

The strangers weren't listening. The man launched himself at Joe, catching him by surprise and wrenching the knife from his hand before any of the others had time to react. He spun Joe around and held the blade to his throat with shaking hands, standing behind him. The woman moved closer, wide eyes flitting between Violet and the others.

"Don't move," the man hissed.

Jack spoke softly. "Take it easy."

"We just want to go!"

"You can—just put the knife down."

"We can't trust them," the woman muttered, shaking her head. "Kill him, Jonny!"

"Oh yeah, then how do we get out of here?" Jonny spat.

"Excellent point," Joe said, gently.

Violet took a small step forward. "Just let him go. You can keep the knife."

"We will." Jonny's eyes flicked across the group, resting on Lex. "We want the axe, too."

"No." Lex's tone was cold.

"Give me the axe!"

"No."

Violet turned to Lex. "Give it to him," she insisted.

"It's mine."

"Sorry to be such an inconvenience," Joe said sarcastically.

"I paid a lot of points for this."

"I'll get you a new one," Jack growled.

Lex scowled, thrusting the axe roughly into the woman's open hand. "Don't trip and cut your throat on it," she said sweetly.

Jonny's eyes swept the group once more, then he pushed Joe away. He and his sister ran from the room, down the stairs, and out of the house.

"WHAT DO YOU THINK THEY WERE TALKING ABOUT?" Violet asked as they drove home. Joe and Lex were in the back with the boxes of chickens, while she sat in the front beside Jack.

"What do you mean?" Jack asked, but she could tell he knew exactly what she was talking about.

"That stuff about our people taking theirs, kidnapping them."

"They were crazy; it was all just crap."

"They knew Ezra's name."

He sighed. "I don't know, maybe they heard us say it earlier?"

Violet tried to recall if they'd mentioned Ezra at all, but her memory failed her. She supposed it was possible, but it still didn't add up.

Jack continued. "They were scared. They've probably been without food and water too long. Stop worrying about it. Let's talk about something else."

Joe piped up from the back. "Okay, how about Lex acting like she cares more about her axe than my neck?"

Lex rolled her eyes. "That's not what I was doing."

"No?"

"No. It wasn't acting. I *do* care more about that axe than your neck."

"Touching."

"Lex," Jack scolded.

She sighed. "They weren't going to kill you, Joe. The guy had one knife, and there were five of us, all armed, standing between him and the door. He freaked out and made a mistake. We should've just said no. He wouldn't have hurt you, and I wouldn't have lost the one thing I care about."

Joe considered this for a moment. "I get it."

She looked skeptical. "What do you get?"

"You like me."

"Where did you get *that* idea?"

"You just said it—'I wouldn't have lost the one thing I care about.' You're afraid to lose me."

"No, you idiot, I meant I wouldn't have lost my axe if we'd just stood firm."

But Joe was shaking his head. "I finally understand. The sarcasm, the stern expression, the way you always make fun of me. You actually *enjoy* being in my company."

"No. No, I don't."

"Are we... are we becoming friends?"

"Absolutely not."

Joe grinned at Violet. "We definitely are."

Scowling even more than usual, Lex reached for the box at her feet. "Okay, *friend.* Here." She opened the lid, releasing the cockerel who'd torn Joe's arms to shreds earlier.

Violet turned back to the front as he cursed loudly, trying to fight back the bird's attempt to inflict further harm. Lex began to laugh.

I guess Joe finally won his bet.

FOURTEEN

WHY ARE YOU STILL EVEN THINKING ABOUT THIS? You're being ridiculous. You're acting like a crazy person.

You're going to get caught.

Despite the thoughts spinning around her head, Violet still wouldn't be dissuaded. She knew she was being stupid. Jack was almost certainly right—the people they found were just a couple of crazies with no idea what they were talking about. She had lived in Harmony for months, and not once had she ever seen anyone 'taken'. There had been plenty of people who'd joined the community and plenty more who hadn't, either because they didn't want to or had tried to kill Violet and her friends the moment they approached. She and the other scavengers had never kidnapped anyone.

But we're not the only ones who leave Harmony?

Violet had suddenly realized she still had no idea what the very highest point holders did. The roles of those who lived in Harmony's best houses were a mystery. They reported directly to Ezra, and left the security of the walls almost as often as she did. What did he have them doing?

That was what had motivated her little afternoon search. For the past half an hour, she had been wandering around Harmony looking for...

What are *you looking for, Violet? People in cages? A sign above a building that says Slaves This Way?*

No. She wasn't expecting to find any of those things. But she had to put her mind at ease, especially now that she'd gotten herself worried about it. The strange thing was, although the excursion had been motivated by her fear something terrible was going on in Harmony, she was beginning to enjoy herself. She had never taken the time before to simply walk around the community, despite living there for so many months. Usually she was hurrying to get food, to get ready for a run, or to get back home before dark. Today, it was like she was seeing the place properly, finding out so much about the community in which she lived.

She learned, for example, that the lowest point holders showered outside. While she and her friends had their own bathroom, those without could use the communal showers in the warehouse. She didn't know until today, however, that they cost one point per use, and so those who were low saved precious funds by showering outside with buckets. She watched now as several children ran around excitedly while their mother tried to tip a bucket of water over their heads. They were all laughing.

Violet also learned that there was a woman living in the shacks who rescued animals. Outside her home were various cages filled with what she assumed had once been beloved family pets: rabbits, a couple of guinea pigs, three cats—one of whom was heavily pregnant—and even a parrot. She wasn't selling them—just liked having animals around.

But the most shocking thing Violet learned on her travels was that the mean old woman who ran the clothing stall had a boyfriend.

'Boyfriend might be pushing it. She's got a so-old-he-looks-like-a-dried-up-mummy friend.

During her walk, she'd accidentally stumbled upon the two of them making out. It was horrible. The sound of two pairs of dry old lips smacking together would surely follow her to the grave. When they saw her, they disentangled at once, bones creaking as they did so. Then the woman had stalked past, hissing, "If you tell my husband, I'll kill you."

Violet wasn't sure how a woman with skin reminiscent of an old leather purse and an eye that fell out more often than it stayed in could have a husband *and* a boyfriend, but the old bat was more intimidating than the zombies, so there was no way she would rat her out.

Something far less horrifying that Violet discovered was that there were several areas of the community which were more heavily guarded than others. She was normally in such a hurry that she never thought about why some of Ezra's people were hovering outside certain doors, but now that she was actively searching, she couldn't help but think it was rather odd. Up ahead, Jack was standing outside one of the doors to the main warehouse. It was an entrance she had never used and had never seen anyone else use, either.

"Hey," Jack said as she approached. "How's it going?"

"Good."

"What are you doing?"

Looking for signs that Ezra kidnaps people. "Not much."

He raised an eyebrow. "You're a terrible liar, Violet."

"So I've heard. Fine, I'm snooping."

"Snooping?"

"After what those people said yesterday... I just couldn't get it out of my mind. What if it's true?"

Jack pinched his fingers to the bridge of his nose, closing his eyes with a sigh. "They were crazy. They probably hadn't eaten in weeks. That can make people totally paranoid."

She'd heard all this already. In fact, she'd told herself the very same thing at least ten times, but it hadn't made her feel any better.

Jack sighed again. "So, Ms. Lansbury, what have you found?"

"Ms. Lansbury?"

"...Never mind. What have you found?"

"For starters, the old woman who runs the clothing

stall is cheating on her husband."

His eyes widened. "Crazy-Eye has a boyfriend? How do you know?"

"I saw her making out with another old guy."

"And how was that for you?"

"Absolutely horrifying. I'll need to pour bleach on my eyes later."

Jack grinned. "Anything else?"

"There are a lot of locked doors around here."

Jack raised an eyebrow. "Well, people probably want their privacy. Not everyone enjoys being watched while they make out with their secret boyfriend."

"You sound as though you speak from experience."

"Oh, definitely. My secret boyfriend and I really value our privacy."

Violet snorted. She supposed he could have a point; locked doors didn't mean too much on their own. "What's in there?" she asked, nodding to the one behind him.

"Ezra's place. This is his private entrance, so he doesn't have to go through the dining hall."

"Why does he need it guarded?"

"He likes his privacy, I guess."

"Secret boyfriend?"

"Almost certainly."

Violet smiled, but she still couldn't shake her feeling of unease. Jack looked a little concerned now.

"Hey, stop worrying, okay? You've lived here for months—you know it's safe."

"I know. You're right."

"If it makes you feel better, I'll inform you if I hear any screaming from in here."

Violet, defeated, smiled again. "Thanks."

He winked. "No problem. Listen, I'm glad I saw you. Do you want to meet for dinner later? There's something I wanted to talk to you about."

"Sure."

"Great, I'll see you at guard changeover."

JACK WAS ALREADY IN THE DINING HALL WHEN VIOLET arrived at six o'clock and had picked up a tray of food for her.

"You shouldn't have done that," she protested. "I can use my own points. This must have cost you at least eight." Jack had bought some of the most expensive items—a range of vegetables, a good quality cut of meat, fresh juice, and even a slice of cake for dessert.

If only I could taste any of it.

He shook his head. "It's cool, I've got enough. I'm sure points expire, anyway, so I may as well use them." They didn't, but Violet appreciated his kindness.

"So..." he began, trailing off. His eyes were focused on his own tray as though there were something fascinating hiding in his potatoes.

Is he sweating?

"Are you alright?" she asked.

"What? Yeah. I'm good. How are you?"

"Good."

"Good. We're both... good."

Silence. Violet thought this might have been the most awkward conversation she'd been in for a while, and for once it didn't appear to be her fault.

"Hey guys." Lex slid into the seat next to Jack, and Joe took the one beside Violet, who breathed a sigh of relief at their appearance.

"Wow, Vi, you got cake?" Joe asked, eyes widening. "Wasn't that four points a slice?"

Lex grinned. "Some people don't blow their earnings on ridiculous things, Joseph, so they can afford to spend a bit more on food."

"I do not blow my points."

"Oh really? Why don't you tell Jack and Violet what you just bought?"

Jack's eyes were still firmly focused on his tray, not really listening, but Violet was curious.

"What did you buy?"

Joe's tone was casual. "An alarm-clock radio."

She raised an eyebrow. "But there are no broadcasts anymore."

"I know."

"And you already have a regular alarm clock."

"I know."

"So why—"

"It was a good deal. Sometimes you just have to follow your instincts."

"That makes no sense, but sure."

Lex laughed, and Joe rolled his eyes, pointing his fork in her direction as he spoke. "What I buy is my business. I don't need you following me around picking on every little thing."

"I'm sure, but you're so easy to pick on, and my following you around is punishment for you losing me my axe."

Joe threw Violet a pained expression. "She's not left my side all day."

"Is it driving you crazy?"

"Sometimes people just want some time alone, you know what I mean?"

"Absolutely," Jack muttered.

Lex didn't seem to have heard him, but Joe clearly had. For a moment he appeared to contemplate something, and then he unexpectedly got to his feet. "Lex, let's go sit outside."

Lex raised an eyebrow. "Why?"

"Because... it's nice."

"It's raining."

"What, you've never eaten in the rain?" He pulled a face. "Are you scared? Worried about messing up your hair?"

That was enough. She scowled, getting to her feet. "Let's go. It'll be interesting to see what happens to that thing on your face when it gets wet. Maybe it'll drown."

They headed outside, still arguing, and Jack seemed to relax.

"Are you sure you're alright?" Violet asked. "You're acting kind of strange."

"Yeah, sorry. I guess my mind is somewhere else."

"Anything I can help with?"

"Maybe." Jack paused. "How are things with you and Matt?"

Where did that come from?

"What do you mean?" Violet asked. Her appetite suddenly vanished, and an uncomfortable feeling rose from the pit of her stomach.

He was clearly thinking carefully about the wording of his next sentence. "Joe was telling me a bit about your history. He said how close you were."

"I guess we were. We went through a lot."

"Joe said that you and Matt had a thing."

I'll kill him.

"A 'thing'?"

Jack smiled for the first time since sitting down. "He said that you cared for each other, but both danced around it, and it never really got going."

Oh Joe, how do you want to die?

Violet scowled, speaking through gritted teeth. "Sounds like Joe knows an awful lot about things I had no idea about."

"He wasn't trying to gossip," Jack added hastily. "I asked, and he made me promise not to talk about it with anyone. Especially you."

"How kind of him."

Jack smiled again, eyes flicking back to his tray. "I guess I was being a little nosy."

Violet's cheeks were burning, and she shifted uncomfortably in her seat. The last thing she wanted was to be having this conversation. She hadn't even allowed *herself* to think in too much detail about what she and Matt might've been, so discussing it with someone else, someone who'd not even been there from the start, was a nightmare. Still, Jack was watching her expectantly. She had to say something.

"Matt and I... Matt and I were complicated."

He waited for more.

He didn't look like he was hoping for juicy gossip or something to make fun of her over, he just seemed genuinely interested. She sighed. "No, that's not true. Matt and I were simple—we were friends. Regardless of whether either of us wanted more, nothing happened. Besides, he has Anna, so it doesn't matter anyway."

Jack nodded as though he understood. "Seeing him with her must be difficult."

She didn't answer right away. They were swimming in waters she'd barely allowed herself to dip a toe into before now. "I'm glad he's happy. I'm glad he found someone and wasn't alone out there."

"It's just hard when it's not you."

Ouch. Say it like it is.

But she couldn't help but feel that maybe, just maybe, Jack was right. She'd been so preoccupied with disliking Anna for her beauty that she'd ignored the fact that maybe that wasn't the reason she felt so uncomfortable around her. It wasn't that Anna was gorgeous, it was that she had fallen into a relationship with Matt that Violet had never gotten the chance to explore. She didn't know if she was jealous; it wasn't like she lay awake at night daydreaming of riding off into the sunset with Matt. Or holding hands and cuddling up on moldy old blankets.

Not often, anyway.

Perhaps it was that Anna had something with Matt that would always make her more important to him. She was his girlfriend, whereas Violet was just a friend from his past who'd tried to eat him a couple of times.

That's it. You're not in love *with Matt, you're just sad because he's found someone to fill the space you left.*

That was her answer, and she was sticking to it... though she wasn't planning on discussing this break-through with Jack. Instead, she changed the subject. "Anyway, you said you wanted to talk to me about something?"

He thought for a moment, then shook his head. "Don't worry. It doesn't matter."

"Seriously? You're going to leave me hanging like this?"

"It can wait. Now isn't the right time."

And even though she didn't know what it meant, the uncomfortable feeling in Violet's stomach convinced her to drop it.

THE NEXT MORNING, EZRA GATHERED EVERYONE IN the courtyard. He seemed to be in a more cheerful mood, standing above them confidently, and Violet wondered if he'd figured out who had freed his workers. There were whispers about a couple of people from the shacks who'd disappeared. She wondered if they'd been exiled in secret. That would be unusual, because Ezra usually liked to make a big show of an exile as a way of convincing others to stay on the straight and narrow, but there were occasions when people just vanished. Violet assumed they'd been kicked out for doing something they shouldn't.

"Today, we batten down the hatches," he said to the crowd. "There's a storm coming, and I want everyone securing the fence to make sure it doesn't blow over, covering windows to keep them from shattering, and nailing down anything that can't be taken inside." He glanced over to the scavengers, who were standing to the left of the stage. "I want you guys on one last run before we close up shop. Grab anything you think could be useful. If the storm damages our fortifications, we'll need all hands on deck to clear this place up. There won't be time for supply runs until we know we're secure." He made his way back to the warehouse, stopping to mutter something to one of his soldiers, a woman who immediately headed off in the direction of one of the locked doors with three others. Violet caught Joe's eye, and she could see he was watching the interaction, too.

"He sounds worried," Anna said, moving closer. "Does he really think the fences will come down?"

"I don't know," Violet replied. "They never have before."

Jack joined the group, zipping up his jacket. "We've lost a few panels during storms in the past, but we've never had a really bad one." He peered up at the sky, where thick black clouds were beginning to form. "If Ezra's nervous, we better hurry up."

Jack took them to a strip mall on the outskirts of town that they hadn't yet explored. There was a sandwich store, a coffee shop, a massage place, a camera store, and an ice cream parlor.

They left their cars and gathered out front. Violet noticed that Matt's hair, still refusing to sit neatly, was much shorter. She wondered if Anna had cut it or if he'd scraped together enough points to pay someone else to do it. Either way, he looked good.

Better, *he looks* better.

The clouds above were getting darker, and more than once she thought she heard the distant rumble of thunder.

"We should split up," Jack suggested. "We'll be able to gather supplies more quickly that way."

"No," Joe replied sharply.

"What?"

"No. We have no idea what might be inside these buildings, and we don't have enough people to split into decent sized groups. For once, can we not follow the cliché of every single horror movie and just stick together?"

Jack gave it some thought, then relented. "Okay. Let's work through each of the buildings to make sure they're safe, *then* we'll split up and search for supplies."

"Perfect."

They went to the sandwich place first. The smell of rotten meat hit them like a wave the second they stepped inside. The food on the counter, thanks to maggots and other insects, had festered away to almost nothing, but the stench still lingered, wrapping around them like a heavy blanket. There was a body on the floor by the counter, a bullet hole through what was left of his head. He had clearly been there for a long time, and the maggots were making the most of what was left of his flesh.

Jack knelt beside the corpse, searching his pockets. He pulled out a switchblade, but as he removed it, the body shifted and its head rolled free of its shoulders as though it had never been attached in the first place.

Anna crinkled her nose. "Lovely."

Jack playfully kicked the skull toward Joe, who squealed like a child, before kicking it back. Lex intercepted, sending the skull spinning to Matt's feet. He made to kick it, but Anna took his arm.

"Can we get on with it, please?" She didn't wait for a response, dropping her hold and walking pointedly to the counter.

Matt threw an apologetic glance in Joe's direction before following.

They continued to explore, found no biters, and moved on to the massage place. As they entered, Ryan looked around at the group, pointing with his bachete. "You know, this is like being in a horror movie."

"You just figured that out now?" Matt asked, eyebrow raised. "The zombies never made you think of it before?"

Ryan shook his head. "No, I mean you all make up the classic characters."

"How so?" Violet asked, opening a door behind the counter and glancing inside.

"Jack's the leader, Joe's the funny one, Lex is the tough one. It's so easy."

"Which one am I?"

"You can be the hot girl," Jack answered for him, smiling. "There's always a pretty one."

Violet felt heat rising in her cheeks, but Joe shook his head, furrowing his brows. "Violet's not the pretty one."

"Wow, thanks, Joe," she drawled.

He grinned. "I just mean the hot girl is always dumb.

She just walks into danger or runs up the stairs when she should be heading for the front door. The hot girl always dies straightaway. She has no brains and no talent. You can be the main character, the one who survives until the end."

"Okay, I suppose that's better."

"No problem. Lex can be the pretty one. Ow!" He was cut off when Lex threw a pot of lotion at him.

They continued through the different buildings. All were clear of both dead and survivors. They ended their search in the coffee place. Matt got incredibly excited when he found a donut that seemed to be mold-free, and he held it in the air excitedly.

"Look what I found!"

Anna's eyes widened. "What's it like?"

He tapped the donut on the table in front of him. "Incredibly hard."

"I meant the donut, Matt," she said, grinning wickedly.

The others laughed at the crude reference, and Violet forced a grin across her face, though the whole interaction made the feeling in her stomach bubble back to the surface.

"Okay," Jack said. "I think it's safe. Let's—"

"Split up?" Joe guessed.

"—break into two groups. I'll take Lex and Ryan and go back to where we started. The rest of you start searching in here, and we'll try to meet in the middle."

Jack, Ryan, and Lex headed outside, and Violet watched as Anna and Matt began to search for supplies. She glanced around the tables. There didn't appear to be anything worth taking, but sometimes things were hidden in unexpected places. She headed for the counter, but halfway there, Joe grabbed her arm.

"Violet, a word?"

He took her outside to the empty street.

"What is it?" she asked.

"What's going on?"

"What do you mean?"

"With you and Matt. You looked like you were about to eat Anna when she made that joke."

"No I didn't."

"I'm half-zombie, too. I know that face." His voice softened. "Vi, I love you. You're my best friend. You're like my sister. But you suck at lying. I don't even need you to say it; I already know."

She narrowed her eyes. "Is that why you told Jack about Matt and me?"

Joe seemed genuinely surprised, then guilty. "He told you? I made him swear not to." He lowered his head. "I'm sorry. I wasn't trying to talk about you behind your back."

"I know, but a little warning next time might be nice."

He nodded. "The next time I tell someone about the secret love thing, I'll make sure you know about it."

She threw her hands up in the air in exasperation. "There's no secret love! Matt and I are just friends."

"But the two of you were—"

Violet wouldn't let him finish. She was so angry she couldn't bear to hear another word about what Joe thought the two of them had been. "I'm so sick of everyone thinking they know more about my life than I do! It doesn't matter what we were, Joe. Nothing matters now."

"That's not true, and we both know the longer you deny it, the harder it's going to be. You can hardly even stand to be in the same room as Anna, and you talk to Matt like he's a stranger."

Violet's rage was bubbling over. "What do you want me to say? That I'm jealous? Fine, you win, I'm jealous! Not because I'm *in love,* but because I never got the chance to find out if I could be." She was babbling, the words pouring out without her realizing exactly what she was saying. "Just when I was trying to figure out how I felt for him, he died. Except he didn't die, he was fine—great, actually—and shacking up with possibly the most beautiful woman I've ever seen. He doesn't care about me anymore, and even if I did still think of him like that, it's too late. I lost my chance. He's moved on, and I just need to get over it, because he certainly has." She was out of breath now. "Is that what you wanted to hear?"

"Pretty much. The yelling was maybe a little loud..."

"Hey."

Joe and Violet turned at the same time to see Anna standing in the doorway. "Are you guys coming back in?" Her face was a mask, completely unreadable.

"We'll be right there," Violet answered hurriedly. Anna nodded, heading back inside with a brief smile.

Violet's whole body felt as though it was burning up, legs wobbling as she looked back at Joe. Her heart raced so loudly she could swear it was making the sidewalk tremble. "Do you think she heard?"

"No, she was smiling. She wouldn't have been smiling if she'd heard you say you want to steal her boyfriend."

"I didn't say that."

He winked, failing, as always, to join Violet in her meltdown. "Sure, okay."

"I *didn't* say that."

"No, absolutely. Gotcha." He turned and opened the door for her.

Unfortunately, that was the worst moment they could've chosen to go back in. As Violet's right foot crossed the threshold, Anna slipped, reaching out her arms to stop herself from falling, and cut her hand on a piece of broken glass on the countertop. Immediately, the room filled with the incredible smell of fresh blood, and everything started to get a fuzzy.

"Don't come in," Violet yelled to Joe.

"What's wrong?" Anna asked, holding up her bloodied hand. Violet stumbled backward, her legs lead.

"Violet," Matt threw himself into her, pushing her away from Anna. She hadn't even realized she was already halfway across the room.

How did I get so close?

Though Matt was stronger, it appeared to be taking considerable effort to keep her from Anna, and Violet was vaguely aware that she was snapping her jaws. Anna was watching her as though she were a rabid animal.

Finally, Matt forced Violet out the door and down to the ground outside, telling Joe to get some water and doing everything he could to keep her restrained. She fought less now that she was outside, away from the smell. Things began to lose their soft edges.

Then it was back. Anna had opened the door and was standing in the doorway, still bleeding, eyes wide and accusing. Joe threw the bottle of water to Matt and then turned and ran in the opposite direction. If Violet didn't know exactly why he was running, it would have been funny.

"What's going on?" Anna asked. Her voice sounded far away. Everything was losing focus again, and Violet found herself fighting against Matt once more in an attempt to break free.

"Get out of here, Anna," he ordered. "Get inside now."

He opened the bottle of water and poured the contents on Violet's face.

The smell disappeared, and she stopped fighting, choking a little as the liquid got into her nose. Matt was watching her closely, checking for signs that she was still dangerous. His breath was cold against her wet face. She felt better, in control of herself, and took a few deep breaths. Matt still leaned heavily over her, pinning her down on the hard ground, and Violet was now aware for the first time that she was in some discomfort.

"I'm okay," she slurred. "Get off."

He did as he was asked, climbing to his feet. "I need—" He gestured to the store behind him.

He needs to check on Anna.

She nodded. "Go. I'm fine."

Matt hurried inside. Violet sat up, rubbing her head. The objects around her had all regained their sharp edges, and she could see Joe cautiously making his way over.

"So, this isn't great," he called as he approached.

"Nope."

"Puts the whole 'did she hear us' thing into perspective, huh? I mean, she's probably forgotten all about you liking Matt now that you've tried to eat her."

"Shut up."

The door opened, and Matt came out. "I've cleaned her up, but we need to talk before the others come back."

Slowly, like children being sent to the principal, Joe and Violet followed Matt back inside.

Anna was pacing, running her hands through her

hair. The cut had been bandaged, though the smell of her blood still lingered in the room, making Violet feel slightly light-headed. She could control it, though. She had to.

Anna turned, staring her down. "What the hell *are* you?"

S I X T E E N

THINK OF SOMETHING, AN EXCUSE, A REASON YOU flipped out that's even slightly believable.

Violet sighed. "I'm infected. Like the dead."

Okay, cool. Honesty. I'm sure there will be no follow-up questions to that one.

Joe's eyes widened incredulously. "You couldn't think of *any* lie?"

Anna took a step back. "What does that mean?"

"It means that if I smell or taste blood, I lose control and kill people. Most of the time I don't remember anything—I just wake up later and I'm back to normal. Or sort of, I guess."

"You're one of the droolers? One of those *things*?"

This is going super-well. Awesome choice to tell the truth, Violet.

But she kept going. "Joe is, too. We're both infected."

Joe held up his hands. "You had to drag me down with you?"

Matt turned to Anna. "They're not dangerous."

She scowled, crossing her arms. "Oh really? That's a little hard to believe when she just tried to *eat* me!"

"I wouldn't let that happen. I *didn't* let that happen."

"Does anyone else know?"

"Toby," Joe answered. "Just Toby."

"Not Ezra?"

"No," Violet said.

Anna exhaled, pacing the length of the counter, keeping a sizable distance between herself and Violet. Matt stepped in front of her and took her hands. "Please, Anna. Please don't say anything."

"Matt..." she trailed off, dark eyes locked with his.

"Do you trust me?"

"It's not about—"

"Do you trust me?" he repeated.

"...Yes."

"Then please, keep the secret."

Anna paused long enough to worry Violet, but eventually Anna bit her lip. "Fine." She glanced over at Violet and Joe. "But just so we're clear, both of you stay the hell away from me."

THE RIDE BACK HOME WAS MORE THAN A LITTLE AWKward, but for now at least, Anna was keeping her word. Jack, Ryan, and Lex were completely unaware of what had happened.

Ten minutes into the journey, the clouds turned black and the first drops of rain began to fall on the windshield. By the time they arrived back at Harmony, those raindrops had become a downpour, and the thunder was rumbling regularly. Back in their apartment, Violet headed to the bedroom. She needed time alone to think.

Throwing herself down on the bed and unsettling Ben who'd been curled up on top of the blankets, she ran her fingers over her scar in an attempt to calm herself. Unfortunately, it wasn't working. Images from the day raced through her head, and she buried her face in her pillow, groaning loudly.

"Feeling good?" Joe asked as he entered the room, closing the door quietly behind him. She groaned again in response, not even bothering to raise her head. He threw his pillow at her, so she turned, lying on her back and staring up at the ceiling.

"Could've been worse," Joe said from his bed.

"Matt's girlfriend almost certainly heard me talking about how jealous I am of her, which would've been bad enough if it weren't for the fact that I almost ate her immediately afterward. How could it possibly be worse?"

"I don't know... you could've had toilet paper under your shoe the whole time."

Violet felt the corners of her mouth twitch. "Yeah, that would've been awful."

She supposed maybe Joe was right—not about the toilet paper thing specifically, but rather about how things could've been even more terrible. Though she'd come close, she'd not eaten anyone today. Sure, Anna knew her secret, but so far, she'd kept it to herself.

She glanced up at the window as the rain hammered against the glass. There was a flash of lightning in the distance.

"Do you think this will go on all night?" Joe asked.

"Maybe."

Maybe it'll be so bad Anna will forget all about me being infected.

"I hope there aren't any tornadoes," he murmured.

Maybe Anna will get sucked up inside one and I'll never have to deal with her again.

"Yeah, me too," Violet replied unconvincingly.

Joe began to rummage around in his bag. "I almost forgot, I got you something." He pulled out a Polaroid camera. Violet's eyes widened, and she grabbed it excitedly.

"Are you serious? When did you find this?"

"Today, just after our little coffee-shop experience. I guess one of their hipster customers left it behind when things started to get too 'zombie'. I checked, it's got film."

Violet grinned from ear to ear and celebrated by sitting next to Joe and taking a picture of the pair of them. It printed out instantly, and she tacked it up in one of the gaps on her wall.

"I love it," she said. "Thank you."

"Come on, let's show the others."

They spent the next few hours in the kitchen with their friends, talking, playing board games, and taking pictures. In fact, Violet was almost feeling relaxed when there was a knock at the door. Joe answered. It was Matt, soaking wet and smiling.

"Hey, great news—the chickens have escaped."

Joe raised an eyebrow. "How?"

"No idea. Flew, I guess?"

"Apparently chickens don't fly."

"What? They have wings."

"So do penguins."

"Yeah, but chickens are—"

Violet interrupted, getting to her feet. "What do we need to do?"

Matt ran his hand through his wet hair. "Right, sorry. One of the soldiers told me they got out of their coop. Apparently, they're kept just outside the wall. He said I should go and get them. I guess he thought because I don't have many points that I'd be willing to do anything."

"And you wanted to drag us into the nightmare beyond the wall with you?" Joe asked. "Awesome, thanks."

Matt smiled. "You don't have to come."

Joe shook his head. "No, it's fine, but we'll need to be fast and we have to make sure someone is covering us out there." He turned to the rest of the group. "Any takers?"

"Leave the chickens," Lex said, shaking her head. "Going out there in this weather is suicide. There's got to be zero visibility."

"Let's just do it," Violet said, grabbing her coat.

They got some plastic boxes for transporting the birds, then made their way to the front gate, where two of Ezra's soldiers were waiting.

"Are we sure this is a good idea?" Joe asked one of them. "We're not meant to go out at night, and it'll be harder for you to cover us in this rain."

The tallest soldier, Harding, shrugged. "If we don't get the damn birds now, there's a good chance we'll lose them for good or they'll die in the storm."

Joe raised an eyebrow. "You're not worried about *us* dying in the storm?"

"Let's see if you do, and then I'll let you know if I'm worried."

"How comforting."

Harding grinned. "We'll keep you safe, don't worry."

Violet hoped he was right, because neither she nor her friends were carrying anything more than a knife. They wouldn't be able to hold crowbars or bats along with the boxes for the chickens, so they had to depend on the soldiers for protection.

While two opened the gates, Harding and another took positions in the guard towers on either side. Violet, Matt, and Joe stepped out. The wind whipped furiously around their faces, and Violet could barely see a thing through the heavy rain. They walked for a little while in the direction of the animal pens, and soon they caught sight of the escapees. The flock hadn't gone far; the poor things were stumbling around, confused and bedraggled in the downpour.

"Just get as many as you can," Joe yelled above the howling wind. "We're back inside in ten minutes."

Violet and Matt nodded, and together the three of them began to round up the birds. It was relatively simple; the creatures were soaking wet and terrified, easy enough to grab hold of and cram into boxes. Violet could hear Matt saying something just behind her and turned around to hear him better.

"What did you say?"

"I said, I never thought I'd be outside in a storm in the middle of the night, collecting chickens with two zombies."

She laughed, pushing her wet hair out of her eyes as the wind picked up again. They were all soaked to the skin already. The rain was icy cold, and Violet shivered as she scanned the area. She couldn't see any more birds, even though there had to be at least five unaccounted for.

"Let's go back," Joe called over, reading her mind. Violet and Matt agreed. They'd done enough for now and could come out tomorrow to round up the stragglers. She just hoped the poor creatures had found somewhere dry to ride out the storm.

They began to head back to the gates, but the sound of gunfire soon stopped them in their tracks. Violet saw the soldiers in the towers firing at the dead. There were at least ten of them hammering their rotting hands on the closed gates. Joe swore, only just audible over the next rumble of thunder.

We're trapped out here.

It's okay, at least the dead haven't seen—

The scream of a zombie interrupted Violet's comforting thought. It, alongside the others at the gates, turned and began running straight for the three of them. They dropped their boxes and sprinted in the other direction, but their getaway was difficult for a number of reasons. They were wearing soaking wet clothes, the rain was so heavy it was hard to see anything clearly, and because Violet had managed to survive a year of the zompocalypse without managing to improve her cardio ability one bit.

"In here," Matt cried above the sound of the storm and screams behind them, pulling her into a nearby building. Joe was already inside. They ran through the dusty hallways and up the metal stairwell. Violet was already exhausted, but Matt kept hold of her hand, pulling her along so she had no choice but to keep moving. They burst through the doors at the top of the stairs and out into a long hallway lined with doors on either side.

"I can still hear them," she panted. The dead were close, already in the building.

Joe headed for a door at the end of the hall on the left-hand side. "It's an emergency exit, we can get out this way," he said over his shoulder as he hurried through.

Violet and Matt made to follow but were cut off by a biter appearing in the open doorway just before Joe's, blocking their path. Matt flung open a door to their right, pulling Violet inside and slamming it moments before the zombie reached them. Seconds later, there were more hands pounding against the wood. The rest of the dead were now outside. Matt locked the door, and though it shook, it stayed closed. He backed away, watching it cautiously.

"They're not getting in, for now at least," he muttered.

Violet allowed herself to breathe, checking out their surroundings. There were a couple of dust-coated desks and chairs, but not much they could use. Certainly no decent weapons. There was a door on the far wall, but when she tried the handle it was locked. The windows were locked, too, but even if they hadn't been, Violet didn't like their odds of surviving the sheer drop to the concrete below. As it stood, she and Matt were trapped. She just had to hope Joe could get away and bring back help, though the chances of the soldiers coming to rescue them during the storm were slim.

"I guess we're not going anywhere for now," she said, dropping into one of the leather desk chairs and sending up a cloud of dust. She swiveled from side to side absent-mindedly for a while, then began to push herself around the room on its squeaky wheels.

Matt raised an eyebrow. "Having fun?"

"Got to pass the time somehow."

"Sure, or we could talk."

She stopped moving the chair around. "Okay." She waited for him to start, but all that followed was silence. "What do you want to talk about?"

Matt thought for a moment. "I don't know..."

Another silence.

Well this is incredibly awkward.

Violet hated not knowing what to say to him. Conversation had always come so easily in the past. In the months they had been together, they'd talked for hours about everything and nothing. In the times they hadn't spoken, the silences had felt comfortable. Nothing like this. She busied herself by wheeling around again on the squeaky chair.

Matt sat down heavily on one of the others. "I don't remember it being this hard before."

She shook her head. "It wasn't."

"Anna said maybe it's been too long."

Oh did she? Well isn't she so clever and awesome?

"Really?" Violet asked, trying to keep her tone even.

"Yeah. She said we've been apart so long we might find it hard to get back to how it was. If we ever can."

"Right."

"She says people change, and with things how they are, they change even more. Someone you were close to only a few months ago could be a completely different person now—"

"Well, if that's what Anna thinks..." Violet muttered, her tone cold.

He raised an eyebrow. "What?"

"Nothing." She spun in lazy circles, the chair continuing to squeak with each rotation. Matt got to his feet and moved toward Violet, forcing her chair to a stop.

"Do you have a problem with Anna?"

"What? No."

He clearly didn't believe her. She didn't blame him; she didn't think anyone with ears would've been convinced by her attempt at sounding genuine.

"What is it?" he pressed.

She shrugged like a moody pre-teen. "Nothing."

Matt turned away from the chair in frustration. "You don't talk to me anymore."

"What? We're talking right now."

"You know what I mean. You're doing that thing—you've done it ever since we found each other again..." He searched for the words. "You're so closed off. You never used to be like this. We used to be—"

"That was a long time ago. Things have changed. *We've* changed. Just like *Anna* said." Violet said her name like it was a terrible curse word.

"That's not what she meant. Anyway, I haven't changed."

No, you just walk everywhere hand in hand with your girlfriend, letting her giggle all over your shoulder. Sure, you're the same.

The sudden influx of angry thoughts frightened her a little. Where was all this bitterness coming from? She thought she'd gotten a handle on the whole Matt thing.

Working hard to keep her tone light, she replied, "It doesn't matter. I'm fine. *We're* fine."

The zombies outside hammered even louder on the door. She groaned, leaning her head back. "Well, other than nearly being eaten alive."

But Matt ignored this. "Ever since I came back, it's like you don't know me. We barely talk, and when we do, you're really... awkward."

Violet's eyes widened. "Have you never met me before? I was always awkward."

He shook his head, running his hands through his hair. "No, it's like you don't know how to just be normal."

"Again... this is me."

A small smile played on his lips, but she knew he was frustrated. He sighed. "What happened? I know things are different now—I have Anna, and you have—"

But Violet didn't get to hear what it was that she had because the shaking of the door became even more intense. It sounded as though it were seconds away from bursting open. There had to be more biters out there. Matt went to the door on the other side of the room.

"I've tried; it won't open," she said.

He rattled the handle. "Maybe we could..." He trailed off, looking up at the lock she had failed to notice. He turned it, then pulled the door open easily, glancing back at her with an eyebrow raised.

Of course. Don't even look for a lock, Vi.

She hurried over, and Matt slammed the door shut behind them as the dead burst into the room.

That was too close.

Violet took a step forward. And fell through the floor.

S E V E N T E E N

THE FLOORBOARDS BROKE BENEATH HER, AND SHE only just managed to grab onto them as she fell. Legs dangling through the hole, she held on for dear life. Her arms felt as though they were on fire. Matt was trying to secure the door but turned around at the sound.

"Violet!"

She lost her grip, falling into the room below and landing heavily on her ankle. Something crunched, and Violet screamed in pain and, no longer able to hold herself upright, toppled onto the cold floor. Matt appeared at the hole in the ceiling.

"Are you okay?" he called.

"What do you think?" She tried to get to her feet, but it was impossible to put any weight on her ankle. Slowly, she hobbled over to a box and sat down. The pain was intense and sharp, as though somebody had poked a hot knife through her skin.

"What can you see?" Matt asked.

"Not much." The room she had landed in appeared to have been used for storage. It was full of stacks of cardboard boxes and some built-in shelving units against the walls. There was only one door leading out, and no windows. "There's a door."

"See if you can open it."

"I can't walk, Matt."

"Then hop!"

Violet muttered angrily but got to her feet, slowly and gingerly making her way across the room. She reached for the handle and pulled the door open. A smile spread across her face, and she turned back to the hole in the ceiling. "It's unlocked!"

She turned back just as two biters arrived. Violet made to slam the door but was too slow. The biters pushed against it from the other side, and Violet struggled to keep her balance while trying to close the door. She wasn't strong enough to force it shut, and the two of them continued to throw their weight against the wood.

"Violet!"

She could hear sounds from the room Matt was in. The dead were still trying to get in there, too. It wouldn't be long before they broke down his door just like the other one. But there was another way out of his room, she'd seen it just before she fell. Matt could still escape if he was fast.

"Get out of here," she instructed, working as hard as she could to keep the biters out.

"What?"

"There's a way out. You can go."

"I'm not leaving you."

"No. You can't take them on, not with one knife. I can't fight anyway. If they get into the room with you... You need to run."

"I'm *not* leaving you."

"You don't have a choice!" Violet screamed, sweat pouring down her face. The door swung open a few more inches, knocking into her face, but she pushed it back with all her strength, whimpering at another sharp pain in her mangled ankle. Blood trickled from her nose down to her chin. Matt made no sound, and when she chanced a look at the hole in the ceiling, he wasn't there. He'd gone, just like she told him to. She knew it was the right choice. Even if he managed to get down there without breaking his own ankle, or worse, he still didn't have anything more than his knife to protect the pair of them with. There was no way out of this room other than the door the biters were throwing themselves against. It would just mean two of them dying rather than one. She couldn't watch Matt die, not again.

Her brain began to whir, a thousand voices yelling instructions.

Just let them in.

No, keep fighting!

Climb on the boxes and get through the hole!

Sure, I bet the dead will wait patiently while you hobble around piling boxes up.

Just let them in, get it over with.

There was a sound behind her, and Violet glanced over her shoulder to see Matt getting to his feet. He ran for the door just as one of the biters managed to get its face inside. She could hear more of them coming now, piling up behind the first two. Matt used all the strength he had to force the door closed, decapitating the rabid woman. As soon as it clicked shut, he twisted the lock.

Violet could still hear the zombies trying to break into the room above. Matt answered her unasked question, panting. "I blocked the door. We're safe."

But she didn't feel relieved, she felt angry. She hobbled over to Matt and pushed him. It seemed to hurt her more than it hurt him, and she stumbled back several feet on her bad ankle. He went to help, but she held up her hands, not letting him get close.

"That's your fault," she scowled.

"Huh?"

"That! My ankle."

"But you pushed me."

"I pushed you because I'm mad at you!"

"Okay... Can I ask why? Or would that make you angrier?"

Violet felt her face burning. "Why did you do that?"

"What?"

"Why did you come down here?"

Matt looked genuinely confused. "Why wouldn't I?"

"You could've died. Just a couple of seconds more and they would've been inside; then you'd be dead."

"You needed help."

"You could've escaped. Now we're both trapped." For some reason, she was insanely angry at Matt's reckless choice to save her, even though it had worked. She'd wanted him to get away. She'd wanted him to be safe. Now they were stuck in the tiny room with zombies blocking the only door out. "I don't get it. Why did you do it?"

Matt shook his head in disbelief. "You know why."

"No, I don't. You should've left me."

Don't be ridiculous. Would you have left him? Or Joe? Or Toby? If the situation were reversed, you'd have done the same thing.

She sighed, finally lowering her voice. "I know we're friends... but you shouldn't—"

But Matt didn't let her finish. He took a step forward and pulled her close, kissing her gently on her bloodied lips. Violet felt like the floor had dropped out from beneath her again, which wouldn't exactly have been unexpected in this wreck of a building. Everything was spinning. It was like an electric spark was shooting through her entire body, which hurt in the most exquisite way. Matt put one hand on the side of her face, stroking her cheek with his thumb as he kissed her. She felt like she was home. The door beside them continued to rattle. They wouldn't be able to get out of this room, but right now, she didn't care. Right now, she never wanted this moment to end.

"Well, this is awkward."

Violet and Matt broke apart at the sound of Joe's voice. He was peering down through the hole in the ceiling with a smile on his face. "I thought I'd come and rescue you, but I can come back later if you'd prefer."

Matt grinned sheepishly, while Violet prayed for the ground to swallow her up.

"Good to see you. How's your evening going?"

"Not as well as yours, it seems." Joe lowered a rope through the gap. "I've tied this up. It should be strong enough to climb."

Violet gave the rope a tug, then held it out to Matt. "After you." She wanted to avoid Joe's questioning as long as possible, her cheeks still burning with embarrassment.

Matt gritted his teeth. "I always sucked at this in gym."

He took hold of the rope, groaning as he pulled himself up. For someone who was supposedly terrible at climbing, he ascended in record time.

Violet jumped at a loud bang on the door behind her. Luckily, it was still secure. The dead weren't in yet, but she didn't have long.

"Come on, Vi," Joe said.

"I don't think I can climb with this leg."

"Then climb with your arms."

She gave him a scathing look, and he quickly relented. "Okay, not in the mood for jokes, gotcha. Just hold onto the rope, and we'll pull you up."

She did as she was told. When she was close enough, Joe and Matt each grabbed her under the arms and helped her through the hole.

"What happened?" Joe asked.

"It's my ankle. I fell through the floor and landed on it."

"Can you walk?"

The banging on the door behind them got even louder. Violet sighed. "I guess I don't have a choice."

"I'll help you," Matt said, lifting her arm over his shoulder. Joe took the other, and the pair of them helped their hobbling friend through the door on the other side of the room.

"How did you find us?" Matt asked.

"I looped back around and just followed the sound of the dead. I figured if you were with Violet, the zombies wouldn't be far away."

"Thanks, Joe." Violet was working hard to stay upright, finding that even walking with support was uncomfortable. She hoped nothing was broken—medical care cost a lot of points. That, plus the fact that she was notoriously terrible at running from the dead with two working legs, meant that a mangled ankle was the last thing she needed.

They headed down a different set of stairs in the building, located around the back, moving as quickly as Violet's injury would allow. The wind was still howling when they got outside and the rain felt like thousands of needles against her face, but there was no sign of the dead, so they hurried toward the gates.

MORNING CAME, AND VIOLET'S ANKLE WASN'T TOO BAD AT all. Joe and Matt had insisted on paying for the doctor to come and examine her, and he had found no broken bones. After icing it all night, she was feeling confident enough to take a short walk around Harmony. She wanted to check out the damage after the storm.

If she were being honest, checking out the storm damage was only one of her reasons for wanting to get out of the apartment. Matt had gone back home after the doctor left, and she needed to talk to him. Thanks to Joe's interruption, they hadn't exactly left things on the clearest of terms, and though Violet dreaded having a conversation that involved the words 'so do you *like me* like me?', she at least wanted to know where she stood.

Things were made more difficult when Joe insisted on going with her. She hoped she'd be able to find a distraction for him long enough to give her and Matt a chance to talk.

The damage to Harmony wasn't too bad. A couple of fence panels were leaning slightly, but it was nothing a little reinforcement with struts wouldn't fix. A tree in the courtyard was down and already being chopped up for recycling, and there were a couple of broken windows, but the place didn't look like it had sustained much damage. Apparently there had been a tornado, but it hadn't touched down anywhere inside the compound. Most of the work today involved either taking down the extra fortifications that had been applied to windows and doors or clearing up the debris.

"Morning," Matt said brightly as they approached his shack. He appeared well rested despite their stressful evening, unlike Violet, who realized at that moment that she'd yet to even look in a mirror. She felt a wave of embarrassment at the knowledge she almost certainly had blood and dirt from their earlier encounter smeared across her face. Still, Matt's eyes met hers, and he gave her a shy smile. A smile that seemed to say *we should talk.* But in a good way.

Matt may have weathered the storm well, but his shack was barely holding together. Several of the roof panels had blown away, the glass in one of the windows had a large crack running through it, and Violet was almost certain the building itself was leaning to the left.

Joe raised an eyebrow. "The old home sweet home isn't looking too good, mate."

Matt glanced back at the building. "Maybe not."

"I'm not sure you should be staying there. I don't think it'll keep standing much longer."

Matt considered this thoughtfully, eying the building again. "I don't know, it's stronger than it looks. Plus, I added some reinforcements before the storm hit."

"This is the *reinforced* version?" Joe asked incredulously.

"Trust me, I did a decent job. It's strong. This thing could withstand a—" Matt was cut off as a nearby tree fell onto the shack, smashing through the roof and crumbling the entire thing to the ground. He, Violet, and Joe watched in silence as the final metal strut landed neatly on top of the pile.

"I won't insult you by finishing that sentence," he said, wincing at the remains of his home.

"Was Anna in there?" Violet asked.

"No, she's at the market."

"Oh, good."

And the award for Least Convincing Response goes to... Violet Winter!

"You've got to be kidding me!" Anna, who always seemed to know when Violet was thinking playfully murderous thoughts about her, appeared behind them. She dropped a cloth bag she'd been holding in shock. A couple of cans of soup and a single potato rolled out and lay sadly by her feet. "What happened?"

"Well... a tree fell."

"Yes, Matt, I can see that."

"Don't worry," Joe said. "You can come and stay with us. We've got the room."

Matt opened his mouth to speak, but Anna shook her

head. "I'm not sleeping under the same roof as people who want me dead."

"We don't want you dead."

"No, of course we don't," Violet added, again sounding far less genuine than she'd hoped.

Anna raised an eyebrow. "Right. The moment when you almost *ate* me was a complete one-off, I'm sure."

Without waiting for a response, she stormed off in the other direction, and Matt, after giving Violet and Joe an embarrassed smile, followed.

Joe sucked in his breath. "That was awkward." He turned back to Violet. "What do you want to do now? We could see what else survived the storm?"

"No, my ankle hurts. Let's go home."

WHILE THE OTHERS HELPED WITH STORM REPAIRS AND Joe fixed himself a snack in the kitchen, Violet sat on the end of her bed, her mind racing. This whole Matt thing was now more confusing than ever. She had assumed, naively, that the moment she saw him again everything would be clear. He'd tell her he cared about her, she'd say she felt the same, and everything would be happy and simple. And Anna... would be dead or something. What she hadn't expected was that he'd go after Anna and leave Violet on her own to try and piece together what the previous evening had even meant.

Groaning, she leaned back and covered her face with her hands. Joe chose that moment to saunter into the room with a sandwich hanging out of his mouth. He took a huge bite, nodding in her direction. "Hey Viola. What's up?"

She kept her face covered. "Nothing much."

"No? No news?"

She shook her head.

"Oh, okay, I thought you might have some gossip, you know, after I saw Matt with his tongue down your throat yesterday."

Her face flushed a charming shade of magenta, and

she finally removed her hands. "That's not what happened."

"No?"

"No."

"So, what—he was giving you mouth-to-mouth?"

She bit her lip and sat up, trying to fight back a smile. "Exactly."

Joe laughed. "Fine, don't tell me the gory details. I'll just have to use my imagination. That's more fun anyway."

"It's not like it matters." Her shoulders drooped, the smile now gone.

"What do you mean?"

She gestured to the window. "Because he's out there with Anna. Surely if it meant anything, he'd be with me now, right?"

"Don't take it personally. He's a guy."

"Why are men so complicated?"

Joe took another bite of his sandwich, holding up a finger and talking with his mouth full. "No, that's your first mistake. We're not complicated. We're simple, really simple. Well, most of us. *Matt* is complicated."

"I don't get it."

He took a spot on the bed beside her, nudging her shoulder with his own and offering up a bite of his snack. She shook her head, and he shoved the last part into his mouth in one go.

"If you'd kissed me, or Jack, or any other guy in Harmony, we'd happily hold hands and smash zombies for the rest of our blood-filled lives. But Matt's not like us. Try not to get mad at him; the situation with Anna is difficult. He felt guilty about her boyfriend dying, so he just kind of fell into the guy's job. He's probably worried about leaving her on her own—you know how dependent she is on him. Plus, they were alone out there for months. He must care about her, even if he doesn't want to be together. Eventually, he'll find a way to let her down gently."

Violet scowled, skin pricking. "Why does he have to 'let her down gently'? She's not exactly gentle in the way she talks to us."

"Exactly. Think, Vi—what does she know about us

that could cause all kinds of problems?"

Understanding settled over her like an uncomfortable blanket. "Oh right, the zombie thing."

"Yeah. Matt's really got himself into a hell of a mess right now." Joe must've noticed how disheartened she was, because he nudged her again. "Don't sweat it; he'll be back."

Violet tried to take comfort in his words, but however he spun it, she was over here alone and Matt was out there with Anna. It wasn't exactly a great start to a blossoming romance.

E I G H T E E N

MATT DIDN'T COME TO SEE VIOLET THAT AFTERNOON or evening. It didn't do much to reassure her that things were going in the right direction. She tried to keep herself busy, though, and was heading to the dining hall with Joe and Jack the next morning when the bells rang again.

Joe rolled his eyes. "Are you kidding me with this? Does Ezra just like the sound of the bells or something?"

Jack grinned. "I think it's more that he likes the sound of his own voice. Come on, let's just go and see what he wants, then we'll get breakfast."

Everyone gathered around the stage as usual. Violet scanned the crowd for Matt, scolding herself for being so obvious, but she couldn't see him or Anna. Ezra stepped onto the stage with a wide smile on his face.

"Friends, I have some exciting news for you all." He paused, as if waiting for someone to ask what the news was. As usual, no one said a word. He continued. "Tomorrow night we're going to be holding a special celebration for one of our most prominent trade partners. We will host Jacob and a small group of his people here. We're gonna feed them and fill them with the best wine we have, and all of you get to eat for free, no points needed!"

159

There was a cheer at that news. Getting to eat without spending points was a big deal, and Violet saw some of the skinnier children hopping up and down with happiness. Ezra had only offered this reward once before, and she remembered how the kids from the shacks had spent the evening filling their bellies for the first time in weeks.

She found it difficult to get excited about the party, however, because now there was only one thing on her mind.

What exactly do we have to trade?

She'd never heard anything about trade partners before, and although she had assumed there were other communities like Harmony, had yet to come across one. How had Ezra kept these dealings secret for so long? As one of the scavengers, shouldn't Violet have some idea what they were trading? It certainly wasn't any of the stuff she and her friends found. Those things were always taken straight to the warehouse and distributed through the markets. The words of the people from the farmhouse came flooding back to her. Had Ezra's men really been loading survivors into trucks? Were they trading people?

Stop it, that's crazy.

Ezra was still talking, giving jobs to everyone—he wanted the place sparkling for their guests, and all scavengers were to go out in search of food and alcohol right away.

"Oh great," Joe muttered sarcastically. "That stuff never gets looted. Should be really easy."

As Ezra made his way offstage, Violet turned to Jack, who was wearing a slightly confused expression. "What do we trade?" she asked.

"Beats me. I didn't even know we had trade partners until just now."

Joe piped up. "Maybe we're trading all those people the Crazerson Twins said we keep stealing?"

Violet slapped him gently on the shoulder, uncomfortable with him voicing her own secret thoughts so openly. "Don't say that."

"I'm sure it's just clothing and food," Jack said. "Come to think of it, we grow a lot of crops outside the walls, it's probably that. Let's get moving; you heard what he said, we need to go out."

It was a smaller scavenging group today. Lex was busy, and Toby couldn't get clearance to leave because they were heading closer to the city, which was more dangerous. They drove out of Harmony all crammed into one car together. Jack and Joe in the front, with Anna, Matt, Ryan, and Violet in the back. Anna sat between Matt and Violet and kept playfully whispering in his ear and giggling. She draped her arm over his shoulder, fingers skittering across his neck every now and then. Violet gritted her teeth and attempted to focus instead on the world outside the window.

They rarely ventured anywhere near the city. Though it was still relatively full of supplies, it was a labyrinth of blocked roads, wild dogs, and huge rats. It was usually heavily populated by the dead, though so far on this trip they'd not seen any. She supposed the zombies went wherever the people were, and anyone who'd been living in the city had long since left or been eaten.

They passed different storefronts, of which every window had been smashed and anything worth taking had been taken. There were bones littering the ground, all that remained of the people who'd fallen in the early days—those who hadn't gotten back up again, anyway. She watched as a pack of wild dogs darted into an alleyway in the distance. They'd once been people's pets. Strange how quickly even the cute little fluffy ones reverted to their natural state. Many of them still wore collars, the only reminder of the lives they had once lived.

Violet hadn't had too much trouble with wild dogs. Most of the time they fled from humans. They'd learned to fear them, and rightfully so. While she would never do it, most people weren't opposed to hunting them for food.

She had been chased once by a pack, led by a large, wolf-like creature that had to have been wild much longer than a year. She'd managed to lose them before they got too close, but had been more cautious around dogs outside the walls ever since.

Jack was taking the scavengers to what had once been

a nightclub. It had apparently not been looted with the others because its whereabouts were known only to members. It was located below a tired-looking laundromat, invisible to all except those who knew it was there.

They parked, and Violet followed the group into the deserted laundromat. The sky was a bright, clear blue, as though the storm had blown away every cloud for miles. Sunlight poured into the building, so she stowed her flashlight for now. Washers and dryers lined the walls, and empty baskets were stacked on top of a bench by the window. One of the machines had its door open, and clothes spilled out, dangling down to the floor as though someone had been interrupted halfway through collecting them. Violet briefly wondered where that person was now. Had they been bitten right in the middle of doing laundry? Or had they managed to escape during the chaos?

The sound of the front door closing drew three biters from the back room. They screamed, running toward the group ravenously. Jack easily took out the closest with his crossbow, and Joe killed the next with his crowbar. The third, a skinny woman missing a large chunk of hair, ran for Anna and Violet. Anna stepped aside neatly, leaving Violet to deal with the biter alone. She lodged her crowbar through the creatures' eye, forcing it to the ground.

Don't break a sweat, Anna. I've got it.

Anna surveyed Violet coolly, then gave a dry smile. "Sorry, I thought it might be an old friend."

Jack pulled his crossbow bolt out of the biter he'd killed, then stood up straight, stretching his back. "An old friend?"

"Just a private joke." Anna smiled.

Violet tried to mirror it, but inside she was furious.

For someone who's so afraid I'm going to eat her, she should really stop making it so damn appealing.

The group continued to the back of the laundromat, through the door from which the dead had appeared. There they found a narrow staircase leading down into the dark.

"Well, this looks super inviting," Joe muttered.

Violet noticed out of the corner of her eye that Anna

moved to hold Matt's hand, but he stepped to the side to avoid taking it. Anna brushed it off, acting as though she were just stretching, but her smile had disappeared. Violet couldn't help but feel a little better about that.

They turned on their flashlights, heading down into the darkness. Jack knocked the wall with his crossbow as they walked, trying to tempt any dead stragglers to the stairs. Fighting in the light with their current height advantage would be a lot easier than in the dark. None came, however, so Violet felt relatively sure there weren't any down there.

At the bottom of the stairs, the room opened up. Based on the size, it must have run underneath at least three of the buildings on the street. The group shined their flashlights around, revealing a dance floor, a bar, some booths with tables, and a couple of other doors leading to bathrooms. Jack and Joe headed straight to the bar, calling over excitedly when they found a large supply of alcohol. She and the others milled around the tables, picking up anything else worth taking. Violet found several unopened bags of chips, some cigarettes, and a few more bottles of wine.

"What do you make of all this?" Matt asked. She started, not realizing he was right behind her.

"Make of what?"

"This whole party thing. Do you know what we trade with these people?"

"No, I didn't even know we *had* anything to trade."

"Why do you think Ezra wants to throw them a party? What's he trying to do?"

"Impress them, I guess? I don't know, Matt." She didn't say what she was really thinking—that the whole thing was weird and made her feel uneasy. She couldn't shake the idea that something bad was about to happen, but Matt didn't press the matter any further. In fact, she got the feeling he had something else on his mind. He shifted uncomfortably, eyes flicking to Anna, who was adding some beer bottles to her bag. "Listen, about—"

There was a noise from one of the doors at the other side of the room. It sounded like rattling. Everyone froze.

"We should go and check it out," Violet said quietly.

"Matt, I need your help with these bags," Anna called over.

He looked torn. Ryan, at a table close by, came over. "I'll go," he said, and headed over to the door from which the sound had come. Matt glanced at Violet apologetically, then went to Anna. She tried to ignore the feeling of rejection settling in her stomach, and slowly followed Ryan to the bathrooms.

The noise was coming from one of the closed stall doors in the women's bathroom. It rattled as whatever was inside hammered against it. Ryan glanced at Violet, grinned, then knocked on the door.

"Are you going to be long?" he called, and the banging from within got louder. Nodding to one of the other stalls, he said, "I'll get it from over the top, just keep its attention focused on the door."

He moved over to the stall next to the one with the biter inside and climbed up onto the toilet seat. Violet banged on the door to try to keep the attention of the zombie while Ryan leaned over the thin wall, reaching down with his knife.

The biter continued to pound on the wood, but then all too suddenly it stopped. Ryan's scream cut through the air, and she darted round to find him stumbling down from the seat, holding his hand, now pouring with blood, to his chest. Eyes widening in horror, Violet ran for the door to the bathrooms, calling out for the others to help. The smell of blood was intense, but the scent of infection was growing stronger and stronger, diluting the temptation. He would turn soon.

The rest of the group charged inside, though while Jack, Matt, and Anna hurried to Ryan, Joe paused at the door with Violet.

"What happened?"

"He got bitten."

Another scream from Ryan, louder this time. She and Joe raced over. Ryan's bitten hand, now disconnected from his wrist, lay the floor. Anna quickly wrapped up the bloody stump at the end of his arm while he continued to whimper. Matt stood over the dismembered hand, his machete dripping with blood. Jack's mouth hung open, and he said nothing at all.

"What happened?" Violet asked, keeping as far from the blood as possible and clasping a hand over her nose and mouth.

"I cut his hand off," Matt answered.

"Yeah, we can see that," Joe murmured, eyes glazing.

"We got to it quickly. Maybe it will stop the infection."

"He could bleed out," Jack yelled, suddenly snapping back to reality.

Matt turned, pointing to Ryan's quivering body. "What other choice does he have? It's this or we put a bolt in his head."

"He's right," Ryan panted, his skin already shockingly pale. Beads of sweat covered his face, and he was clearly working hard to stay awake. "This is my only chance."

Jack stood still, eyes fixed on Ryan, crossbow held tightly in one hand. "How will we know if it worked?"

"It worked," Joe said.

"How could you possibly know that?"

But he was right. The smell of the blood, just noticeable through the thick bandages, no longer carried the dark scent of infection. It was sweet, delicious, and human. Matt had cut out the infected part quickly enough to save Ryan's life.

But of course, they couldn't tell Jack this. "I just know," Joe answered lamely.

Jack was understandably unconvinced. "Let's get him back to the car. We have enough alcohol now, anyway. Matt, sit next to him. If you think he's going to turn—"

"I know," Matt interrupted.

Jack helped Ryan to his feet, supporting him under one arm and leading him from the room. Violet held her breath as they passed. She would give it a few more minutes before following. Though the smell of his blood was muffled by the bandages, it was still there, and she needed a break to allow her head to stop spinning.

"That was pretty intense," Joe said, letting out a deep breath. "I suppose bleeding to death is a little better than becoming one of the biters."

Matt wiped the machete on the leg of his jeans as Anna squeezed his shoulder. His forehead was slick with sweat. "We all came into this world kicking and screaming and covered in blood. These days, we have to be prepared to leave it like that, too."

Joe kept his face deadpan. "Great. I look forward to that."

Matt grinned, following Joe out of the room. Violet made to leave, too, but Anna stepped in front of her, blocking the exit.

"Are you okay?" she asked, sounding very much like she didn't care at all.

"Yes, why?"

"It must've been difficult for you, in here with a man who was bleeding out. Must've been very tempting."

"You get used to it."

"I'm sure." Anna glanced at Ryan's decapitated hand on the ground, speaking in a sickly sweet tone. "Do you want that? I'm sure we could bag it up for you to take home. Something to nibble on later?" She smiled, turning and leaving the room before a scowling Violet had the chance to think of a clever response.

Hey Anna, you're the one who needs a hand—keeping your man!

Ugh, too Jerry Springer.

Hey Anna, why don't you shove that hand—

Too obvious.

Hey Anna, I hate you.

Perfect.

N I N E T E E N

"How's Ryan?" Violet asked, taking a spot opposite Lex in the dining hall the following morning. Lex had just come back from the medical building.

"He's doing well. I think Matt saved his life."

Violet exhaled as relief washed over her. "That's great."

"How do you think he knew to do that?"

"No idea. I suppose it makes sense, though."

"I guess so." Lex grinned. "In even more exciting news, check it out." She reached under the table, taking out a brand-new axe with a polished wooden handle and bright red head.

Violet pulled what she thought was a suitably appreciative expression. "Nice axe."

"Thanks. Bought it today. Cost me fifteen points, but it's worth it. Isn't she beautiful?"

Violet had never thought of any weapon as particularly beautiful, but she smiled. "Sure."

"Lex, have you seen Alex?"

The woman, whose name Violet couldn't remember, wrung her hands together anxiously as she addressed Lex. She was tall, slender—verging on skinny—and with brown hair that looked as though it hadn't been washed for a while.

"Alex is missing?" Lex asked.

The woman nodded. "I haven't seen her in two

days. We had a fight. At first, I thought she was just avoiding me until she cooled off, but she's never been gone this long before." She put her hands to her mouth. "What if she left? What if she went outside the wall and something happened to her? She's never been—"

"Calm down," Lex said in a tone that was both firm and reassuring at the same time. "Alex wouldn't leave Harmony; she's not an idiot. She's probably just hiding out until she thinks you've suffered enough. She'll be back."

The woman nodded rapidly but continued to wring her hands. Lex gently took them in her own. "Let me finish eating, and then I'll come and help you search. Okay?"

"Thank you, Lex." She hurried away.

Lex turned back to her food but didn't eat.

"What is it?" Violet asked.

"Nothing. I'm sure it's nothing."

"Ladies." Joe slid into the seat next to Lex, and Jack took the one beside Violet.

"New axe?" Jack asked.

"Yeah, seeing as how Joe lost my last one."

Joe paused, fork halfway to his mouth. "*Lost* it? I almost died..."

"And if you had, I wouldn't have needed to spend fifteen points on a replacement. Think about that next time you decide to get taken hostage."

"Sorry to have put you through that," he replied dryly.

The bells began to ring, and the group collectively groaned.

"I'm so sick of those damn bells," Lex scowled, still holding onto the axe and getting to her feet. The others got up, too, leaving their food behind.

Things had changed a bit out in the courtyard. Ezra's stage was far larger, having been extended on all sides. Violet had no idea when that had happened, but it seemed it was necessary, because he wasn't alone up there today. In all the time she'd been in Harmony, she didn't think she'd ever seen anyone other than Ezra standing over the crowd. Yet today, there were six people on their knees, side by side, behind him. She didn't know any of them personally, but she recognized the faces of a couple of low point holders. They lived near Matt's old shack and often tried to trade for items directly from the truck when she and the others got back from scavenging runs. As she moved closer to the platform, she noticed they each had a rope tied around their neck. These were being held by six soldiers, standing behind the stage.

Violet's stomach sank. Nothing she was seeing suggested anything good was about to happen.

As if on cue, Ezra stepped forward and began speaking, his voice somber.

"Friends, this is a terrible, terrible day." He pointed behind him. "Six of our people, our brothers and sisters, have broken one of the golden rules. They stole. They stole a lot. Enough to leave many of us hungry if they hadn't been caught in time." The four men and two women kept their heads bowed. Ezra turned back to the crowd. "The problem is, despite the overwhelming evidence against them, each of these six have chosen to deny their crimes." He paused, walking the length of the stage, then continued. "Now, I'd hate for you all to think I'm acting hastily. Believe me when I tell you that these people have been with my soldiers for some time, who have tried asking them nicely to admit what they have done. Unfortunately, no dice. So, I've been given no choice but to take a more... hands-on approach." As he spoke, six more soldiers marched onto the platform, each standing behind a prisoner. Every one of them held a long pole, with a biter tied by its neck to the end.

Ezra addressed the six people now, eyes glittering. "The rules are simple. My men are going to walk the droolers toward you slowly. You've got until they reach you to untie the knots around your necks. The first five get to live, the last one doesn't. Unless, of course, anyone wants to confess right now?"

Silence.

He shrugged. "Okay then." He held up one hand and snapped his fingers. Slowly, his soldiers approached the prisoners from behind, each led by a biter, pulling desperately at the poles to reach their meal.

"This is a joke, right?" Matt whispered, joining Violet.

"He's not actually going to let one of those things kill anyone, is he?"

"No, I don't think... he's never..." she trailed off. The truth of it was, she didn't really know anything about Ezra. Was he capable of this?

She looked to Jack for reassurance. After all, he should understand their leader better than she ever could, but he simply stood with his mouth slightly open, an expression of horror on his face.

"I don't know," she finally murmured.

No one in the crowd made a sound. The only noise came from the biters panting and snapping their jaws, the soldiers' shoes on the wooden stage, and the heavy breathing of the six people as they tried to escape. The woman on the far right was the first to do it. She scrambled free of the rope around her neck and stumbled to her feet. The soldier with the biter that had been heading in her direction stopped. Ezra motioned for her to get back onto her knees. She did, eyes darting anxiously to the other five prisoners. A tall man with black hair was next, then a woman with orange curls, who reminded Violet of her friend Maggie.

Two more struggled free, and then only one remained, still fighting against his ropes as the biter approached. Violet's heart hammered in her chest. Surely Ezra wasn't about to let someone get ripped to pieces in front of the crowd?

"Enough," he said, almost lazily.

The biter, just inches from the man's head, was pulled back. Five zombies were dragged from the stage, leaving only the one nearest to the last man, and the soldier holding onto it. Violet felt beads of perspiration on her temple.

I knew it, it's okay, he was never going to kill them. He just wanted to scare them.

It was a cruel tactic, but she could live with that. It was better than what she'd thought was going to happen, anyway. There was a collective sigh of relief from the crowd, who watched fixedly as Ezra moved over to the last man, neatly sidestepping the biter as he passed, and then got onto his knees, eye to eye with the prisoner.

"Now, according to the rules of the game, I'm supposed to let that big guy behind me take a bite out of you."

As if it understood, the zombie snapped its jaws excitedly.

"Please," the man sobbed. "Please don't."

"You got something you need to tell me? Something to tell all of us?"

The man nodded, sweat running down his face. "Yes, I did it. I stole from the market."

Ezra smiled, clapping the man on the shoulder and quirking his head to the soldier with the biter, who dragged it off the stage. "See, doesn't that feel better?"

"Y-yes."

Ezra got to his feet, addressing the crowd again. "Friends, two rules were broken here today. We don't steal, and we don't lie. Now, our pal here has begun to atone—he admitted to what he did." He looked at the five people still on their knees. "Anything the rest of you want to say?"

They shook their heads, remaining silent.

He sighed. "These folks, unfortunately, are still choosing to continue their deception. I cannot allow liars in my community. The obvious thing to do is to kick them out and let the droolers have them, but I'm not an unfair man. These people have families, kids who depend on them. I won't banish them from this place, but I need to ensure there's no more dishonesty in our little slice of heaven." He snapped his fingers again, and ten soldiers came onto the stage. They split into pairs, with one standing in front of, and one standing behind, each of the people who'd freed themselves from their ropes.

Ezra spoke softly to the crowd. "Don't forget—this was their choice."

There were sounds of a struggle, a collective scream, and then the soldiers in front of the prisoners stepped aside as a glorious smell filled the air. The smell told Violet what had happened before she saw anything.

They cut out their tongues.

She held her hand over her nose, knowing she couldn't afford to lose control but unable to make herself leave.

Why is Ezra doing this?

Matt took a step back in shock, and Anna, beside him, gasped quietly.

Ezra addressed the murmuring crowd again as the prisoners were dragged from the stage, all clutching their mouths and sobbing as blood seeped between their fingers. "I know that might've seemed a little extreme, but let me explain what happens when people lie and steal. There's not enough food for the rest of us, points become worthless, we fight and kill each other for crumbs, and then the droolers pick us off like one-legged turkeys. Now I'm betting these five will think twice before stealing again." He pointed to them as they stumbled away. His voice was unnervingly calm considering what had just happened.

"Don't worry, the doctor will make sure they don't bleed out, and they'll be back to begging for scraps in no time." He chuckled. "They'll probably just need to use hand gestures or something. Now, I'm sure the rest of you wouldn't even think about stealing, but if that little thought ever decides to creep its way into your heads, remember them. Remember this." He turned back to the man on the stage, the one who had admitted to stealing.

"I don't like liars," Ezra said, pointing to the bloodstains on the wooden floor. The man nodded, face devoid of all color. Ezra put his hand on the guy's shoulder. "I also don't like thieves." With that, he pushed him backward off the platform, where Violet hadn't realized one of the biters had been chained up. The prisoner screamed as the creature tore into him. Seconds later, they were both put down with a shot to the head. Ezra took a deep breath, turning back to the silent crowd.

"Lesson over."

"WHY DON'T YOU COME TO OUR COMMUNITY?" MATT BEGAN as he and Anna sat down beside Joe at their table in the dining hall. *"It's totally safe and awesome."*

"This has never happened before," Violet muttered, her head still spinning.

"I knew Ezra was intense, I just never thought he was

crazy," Joe said.

Jack shook his head. "He's not crazy."

"Oh sure. What just happened was completely rational."

"I'm not saying that, but the man's not crazy. There must've been a reason..."

Lex shrugged. "They were thieves, right?"

Joe threw a piece of bread at her. "So it's okay to cut their tongues out or let them get ripped apart by biters?"

"As long as it's them and not me. They made their choice." She spoke with confidence, but Violet could see the conflict behind her eyes.

"I don't like this," Anna said. She looked at Matt. "I think we should leave."

He sighed. "And go where?"

"Anywhere is better than here, as long as we're together."

That rubbed Violet the wrong way, but it was Joe that spoke up. "No, it took us too long to find each other again. Whatever we do, we do it as a group. Let's at least take some time to plan our next move."

Matt nodded. "He's right. We can't risk all we have, not now."

Anna scowled. "Staying here is a mistake, it's stupid."

"We're safer together."

"Not all of us." Anna's eyes settled on Violet for long enough to make her feel uncomfortable.

She got to her feet, wanting to escape those laser beams before they burned through her skull. "I'm going to lie down. I have a headache."

"Are you okay?" Matt asked.

"Yeah, I just need some rest."

He clearly wasn't convinced, but she headed out of the dining hall before he could ask any more questions. She needed space to think. Yesterday, her only worry was about whether or not she and Matt were going to be together. Now, she had boy trouble *and* psychotic-leader-who-enjoys-cutting-out-tongues trouble. It was a lot to take in before midday.

She was halfway down the hallway to the main doors

when she was grabbed from behind and forced into a tiny storeroom. The smell of bleach and floor polish burned her nostrils, and she felt a mop handle clatter into her head as she was shoved roughly into the dark. The door shut, and after a few seconds, she recognized the outline of the person standing in front of her.

"Anna? What—"

"I know what's going on," Anna interrupted.

"Good, because I have no idea."

"You need to stop."

"Stop what?"

"Stop whatever it is you're trying to do with Matt."

Violet felt her stomach drop to her feet.

How does she know?

Calm down, just act casual.

Unfortunately, her voice became unusually high with each word. "Me? Matt? Trying?"

Good job, that didn't sound weird and suspicious at all.

"You're trying to steal Matt from me," Anna said.

Violet scowled. "Last time I checked, Matt wasn't an object that could be—"

"Shut up. You know exactly what I'm talking about. I always thought you two acted strange around each other, but I just blamed it on you being weird."

"Thanks."

"But ever since the storm he's been acting differently. Something's changed." She stepped closer, forcing Violet against the shelving unit behind her. Boxes and bottles toppled over. Anna's voice was little more than a hiss, her breath hot on Violet's face. "You think Matt would be happier with you? That you know him better than I do? We've been together for months. I know every inch of his body and every corner of his personality. I understand who he is more than you ever could."

"Anna, I don't—"

"Oh please. I see the way you look at him, like a little lost puppy. It's pathetic." She moved back. Violet realized she'd been holding her breath, and finally let it out. Anna may have been slight, but something about her was incredibly intimidating, and she wasn't done talking yet. "I see the way he looks at you, too. He's confused, conflicted. He feels like he owes you something because of your disgusting abnormality."

"Well, I wouldn't say it's a—"

"And for some reason, he seems to find your bizarre personality *charming*."

"That's kind of rude..."

"But you wouldn't work. You'd soon realize that he's only with you because he feels sorry for you, and he'd soon realize that you're dangerous." Something glinted in Anna's hand.

She has a knife!

Violet spoke slowly. "What are you planning to do with that?"

"Oh please, I'm not going to stab you in a closet," Anna drawled, but she stepped closer all the same. "If I ran this knife along my arm right now, what would happen?"

Violet said nothing.

"What would happen?" Anna repeated.

"You know what would happen."

"I want to hear you say it."

"I'd kill you. I'd lose control and become a monster."

"You wouldn't be able to stop yourself?"

"No."

Anna nodded. "And if it was Matt who was cut? Could you stop yourself then?"

"Anna—"

"Could you?"

She was defeated. "No."

Anna slipped the knife back into her pocket. "If you take Matt from me, you're putting him at risk."

"Matt knows what I am. He wouldn't let himself get into a position where I'm anywhere near his blood."

Anna snorted. "You can be sure of that? You can put your hand on your heart and promise me that Matt would be safe with you? That the man I love more than anything in the world would never end up being ripped apart because you're some kind of mutant freak?" Her face was just inches from Violet's now, her tone urgent. "Can you promise me that?"

Violet opened her mouth and then closed it again. She had nothing to say. No matter how hard she worked to protect Matt, if the two of them were ever trapped somewhere together and he got even the tiniest cut, there would be nothing she could do to keep him safe. She and Joe had been injured together more times than she could count on one hand and were just lucky that their blood had no effect on each other. Matt didn't have that luxury. When their whole lives revolved around running and fighting, there was no way she could be sure he would never get hurt.

When Anna spoke again, her voice was surprisingly gentle. "When my boyfriend Luke died, I wanted to die, too. He was the one person who made me feel safe. I never had to worry about anything because he always took care of me. He was strong. But Matt? He didn't just take care of me, he taught me how to take care of *myself*. He wasn't just strong, he showed *me* how to be strong. Matt made me a better person, and while he did it, he made me fall in love with him. And I know he loves me, too." She sighed, as if forcing herself to say the next part. "But he also feels something for you, and that confuses him. Please, please don't risk his life because you have some kind of history." She didn't wait for a response, swiftly opening the door to the tiny room and leaving Violet alone in the dark, vaguely aware that something from the shelf was leaking onto her head.

TWENTY

VIOLET MADE HER WAY OUT OF THE WAREHOUSE IN A daze, spending the next twenty minutes walking a long meandering path in the vague direction of her apartment. All around her, everyone was getting ready for the party. They were decorating the outside of their homes, heading to the warehouse with food, drink, and extra tables. There were even a few people carrying guitars and other instruments. On any other day, she would've been ecstatic about the idea of listening to music, but right now she could think of nothing except Anna's words, still rattling around in her head.

"He feels *sorry for you.*"

"*Can you promise you won't kill him?*"

"*Don't risk his life.*"

"*He loves me, too.*"

She may have disliked Anna intensely, but that didn't mean she wanted to take away the one person in the world she cared about. And all the stuff about Violet being dangerous was true. Being in a relationship with Matt would obviously increase her chances of being alone with him, and being alone with Violet was dangerous for anyone not already infected. If something bad happened to him because of what she was, she would never be able to live with herself.

Talk to Matt.

She shook away the thought. It was a terrible idea. Matt was too good. He'd do everything in his power to make her feel better. He'd reassure her that she wasn't dangerous, when that was the opposite of the truth. Talking to him would make everything harder.

There was also a tiny bit of her that was terrified Anna might've been right when she said Matt just felt sorry for her. What would happen if they started a relationship and she managed not to accidentally eat him, but it still didn't work out? She would have ruined one of her most valued friendships. And that was only the best-case scenario. The worst was that she'd wake up in a pool of Matt's blood knowing the hideous monster within her had been the last thing he'd seen.

No, she wouldn't talk to him about it. In fact, it would be safer not to talk to him at all. Even a casual conversation could result in her blurting it out, so she needed to avoid being alone with him at all costs. That would be tricky, because he was likely to try and seek her out. She needed to find a barrier, a way to create some distance and ensure he stayed with Anna.

She found herself changing direction, heading away from her apartment and across to the other side of Harmony, to where the soldiers' quarters were. Before she could talk herself out of it, she quickly knocked on the blue door.

Despite the fact that almost all of Ezra's soldiers lived there, it was Jack who answered. He was shirtless except for a towel around his shoulders, clearly in the middle of working out. Violet looked at the ground, her cheeks flushing.

"Hey Vi," he said. "What's up?" He cocked his head a little to one side, observing her curiously. "What happened?"

"What do you mean? I'm fine."

"Okay," he paused. "It's just that you have something weird in your hair."

She shrugged. "It's floor polish."

"Right... is that safe to have so close to your scalp?"

"I don't know."

"Oh."

"I didn't put it there, it spilled on me."

"Right."

There was an awkward silence until Violet remembered that she was the one knocking on his door. She probably needed to lead the conversation. "Do you want to come to the party?"

Jack seemed even more confused. "We all have to go, right? That's what Ezra said."

"No, I mean, do you want to come with me?"

"Sure, we can go together."

She shook her head. He was making this harder than she needed it to be. "No, as my... sort-of date."

That surprised him. "Your sort-of date?"

"Yeah."

"How is it different from a real date?"

"I don't know."

He smiled kindly. "What do I need to do?"

"I don't know."

"Well, it sounds really tempting so far."

She smiled for the first time. "I guess... pick me up, tell me I look nice, and make sure I don't have to dance alone."

"It sounds like a real date to me."

"It's not. It's a sort-of date."

"Of course." He paused, as if mulling it over. "Will you wash the floor polish out of your hair first?"

"Don't try to change me."

He grinned, holding up his hands. "It looks great anyway. Sure, I'll be your sort-of date."

"Good."

"Good."

"Great."

"Awesome."

She bit her lip awkwardly. "I'm going to go."

"See you later."

Jack closed the door, and Violet made her way back to her place, telling herself over and over that it was a good plan. If she was spending the evening with Jack, she'd be able to avoid any awkward conversations with Matt. It felt sneaky and horrible, but if he thought less of her because of it, that would be a good thing. He could stay with Anna, and she would know he was safe. Besides, she would probably have a good evening with Jack. He'd always been kind to her, and he knew how to have fun. Sure, he didn't know her secret, and sure, he didn't make her heart do that weird fluttery thing when she saw him, but it was for the best. Anna was right; she and Matt were a disaster waiting to happen.

This was a good idea.

⌇⌇⌇⌇⌇─────────

THIS WAS A TERRIBLE IDEA.

Violet paced her bedroom. What was she doing? Why had she gone to Jack? It was such a stupid plan. She could've just gone to the party alone and found other ways to avoid conversation with Matt. Or she could've stayed at home. Now she'd surely just made everything worse.

But if she were honest with herself, she knew there was no way she'd have been able to avoid Matt all night. She wanted nothing more than to talk to him, so her will-power would probably last no more than fifteen minutes. Staying at home would be no good, either. If she said she was ill, he would just come around to check in on her. Whether she liked it or not, going to the party with Jack was the only way she could be sure to avoid any intense conversations with Matt.

"You look great." Joe stood in the doorway to the bedroom, giving her an approving nod. Violet's dress was nothing special—black, short sleeved, and a steal at only three points. It was plain, but at least it didn't have a garish slogan on the back. Joe was wearing dark jeans and a red shirt. His hair was freshly washed, but Violet didn't notice that because her eye was immediately drawn to his naked upper lip.

"You got rid of Maurice," she exclaimed, sitting down on the bed in mock surprise.

He grinned sheepishly. "Yeah."

"Why?"

"I figured if I got rid of it, Lex would have to work

harder to make fun of me. She'll have to move onto something less obvious."

"Like your personality?"

"Exactly. That should keep her busy for a couple of weeks at least." He quirked his head toward the door. "Are you ready to go?"

"I need to wait for Jack."

"Oh cool, he's coming with us?"

"No, he's... he's coming with me."

Joe took a moment to process that, then raised an eyebrow. "Like a date?"

"Not a real date."

"But I thought you and Matt—"

"No. We're not. We're nothing like that."

"Right... but you can understand my confusion when I saw—"

She cut him off. "That was a mistake. Matt and I are just friends."

He slowly put the pieces together. "So you and Jack are—"

"We're just friends, too."

"Your life is complicated."

"I know."

Joe paused for a minute. "It just kind of *sounds* like a date..."

"Well it's not."

"Okay," he said, holding up his hands. "My mistake." He turned to the door, opening it. "Well, I've also got a non-date tonight, with Lex. I'm thinking I'll take her to dinner, see a movie, try to cop a feel in the backseat of my car on the way home. You know, typical non-date stuff."

"In your dreams," came Lex's reply from down the hall.

He grinned. "See you later."

He left the room, and Violet heard the front door to the apartment close as everyone else left. She had a few more minutes of agonizing over her decision to go to the party with Jack before there was a knock at the apartment door. With a deep breath, she went to answer it.

Jack stood before her wearing a black suit and a wide smile, holding a bunch of wildflowers in his hand.

Is he wearing cologne? That had to cost a fortune.

He cleared his throat. "Let me see if I remember this right. The first part was telling you that you look good?"

"Yep."

"You look good."

"Wow, you nailed that."

"I've been practicing." He winked, then clearly remembered the flowers, thrusting them out toward her clumsily. "These are for you."

Violet took them, cheeks burning. "Thanks. They're lovely." She put them down on the kitchen counter behind her.

"Shall we go?" he asked.

"Why not?"

Try to sound a little more enthusiastic, Vi.

They walked side by side toward the warehouse. It was relatively quiet outside. Despite the festive mood, there were still rules about noise after dark, and the last thing anyone wanted was to draw the dead to the walls. Residents walked in the direction of the warehouse whispering excitedly among themselves or in comfortable silence.

"Something on your mind?" Jack asked as they approached the courtyard.

Violet bit her lip. She couldn't tell him she was currently thinking about seeing Matt, so she settled on sharing the other thing bothering her. "Do you really think we're trading food?"

"What else could it be?" He paused. "You're not still worrying about what those people in the house said, are you?"

She shrugged. "I don't know, it's just weird that we've never heard about any other communities before now."

"That doesn't automatically mean Ezra's some kind of slave trader," Jack replied, not unkindly. "It just means he plays his cards close to his chest." They were at the doors to the warehouse, and he slowed, turning to face her. "Try not to overthink it. I've been in Harmony a lot longer than you, and I trust Ezra. Sure, he might make some... questionable decisions at times—"

"Cutting out tongues," she interrupted.

"Yeah, I'd say that was one of them. But I've never had any reason to believe he would put innocent people at risk." He put a hand on her arm, squeezing it gently. "I'll find out what we trade, okay? And I'll look into what those people in the house said, too."

"How?"

"I'll ask around. Discreetly. If it'll put your mind at ease, then I want to do it."

She smiled, feeling like some of the weight had been lifted from her shoulders. "Thank you."

"No problem. So now you have nothing else to worry about."

If only that were true.

He held out his arm, and together they made their way into the warehouse.

From the moment she stepped inside, Violet was overwhelmed with the sounds of music, conversation, laughter, and high-spirits. The dining hall was almost unrecognizable. Tables had been pushed against the walls and were now groaning under the weight of food and drink piled on top of them. In the middle of the room was a large dance floor, where a sweaty mass was already churning to the music provided by three people playing guitars, two on violins, and one guy playing some sort of box thing that Violet quickly realized was a drum. Streamers hung from the ceiling and across the walls, along with hand-painted banners welcoming their guests. Each light had been covered with either red, blue, or yellow paper and cast a colorful glow around the room.

"I've never seen the place like this before," Violet breathed, taking in her surroundings.

Everyone was having a good time. There were genuine smiles on their faces, and it was difficult to tell the high point holders from the low ones. After a few moments scanning the room, she spotted Ezra right at the back, sitting at a separate table with several men she didn't recognize.

"That must be Jacob and his people," Jack said, reaching over to the nearest table and getting them a couple of drinks.

Violet could see Joe not too far away, dancing with Lex, though calling it 'dancing' was putting it politely. He was certainly moving his arms and legs, but it was neither well-coordinated nor in time with the music. She got the distinct impression he was moving in that way purely to embarrass Lex, who stood in front of him with her arms crossed across her chest. She was saying something, raising an eyebrow as she did so, but whatever the content, it apparently did nothing but spur him on.

"I think Joe's enjoying himself," Jack said, casually placing a hand on Violet's waist as he leaned close enough to be heard over the music.

She nodded, scanning the room for the rest of her friends. Toby wasn't far away, deep in conversation with a couple of the kids from the shacks. Ryan was still in the medical building, missing out on the night's festivities. Violet couldn't see—

"Hey."

Matt and Anna appeared, both holding plates of food. Matt smiled widely, though his expression flickered a little when he noticed the positioning of Jack's hand.

Violet hurried to distract him. "This place looks great, doesn't it?"

He seemed to snap back to the moment. "Yeah. So do you."

"Thanks."

Anna's eyes swept over the black dress. "Is that the right size for you?"

Violet had no idea how she was supposed to respond to that comment. She simply smiled, trying to pretend her cheeks weren't burning. "Yes."

"Oh, sorry." Anna bit her lip as if mildly embarrassed, but it was clear that she wasn't.

Tension hung in the air, and Violet wondered if the guys could feel it, too. She hoped not and tried to turn her focus back to the party. Joe was now even closer to Lex, shimmying up and down in front of her with a bizarre expression on his face. Violet really hoped his moves were part of some elaborate joke; otherwise, his dancing capabilities were both appalling and mildly frightening.

Just as she was about to mention this to the others, Anna grasped Matt by the hand.

"Dance with me," she ordered, not waiting for a response but instead dragging him over to the dance floor. He glanced back, as if trying to send Violet a message, but she didn't attempt to decipher what it was. It didn't matter anyway.

Anna draped her arms over his shoulders, resting her head on his chest despite the fast beat of the song. Violet forced herself to look away, trying to ignore the horrible, wrenching feeling in her chest.

"Do you want to dance?" Jack asked.

"I don't dance."

"Neither do I. Neither does Joe, by the looks of it, but it's not stopped him."

She followed his gaze. Lex was gone now, and though Joe's dancing had dramatically improved, it wasn't exactly in time with the music. Or any music ever created. The crowd was slowly parting around him; however, it soon became clear that giving him more room for his moves was a mistake. High kicks and a possible attempt at the worm were now being incorporated into the routine. Most of the other dancers were watching on with mild amusement, though Matt and Anna were still slow-dancing, and she'd managed to wind herself even more closely around him.

"Excuse me." Violet swallowed her drink in one gulp and turned on her heel, heading for the bathrooms. She needed to get away from all of them, from the noise. She needed to splash some water on her face.

Lex was already in there, sitting on one of the sinks and kissing a pale girl with white-blonde hair. They stopped when Violet came in. Lex grinned, but her partner's eyes widened in embarrassment.

"Great party, right?" Lex asked as the blonde stepped back, readjusted her shirt, and smoothed down her hair self-consciously. "This is Kiera. She's from Jacob's group."

Kiera waggled her fingers awkwardly.

"Nice to meet you," Violet said.

"Yeah, you too." Kiera paused, then glanced over at Lex. "See you later," she mumbled, then scuttled back out to the party. Lex hopped off the sink and began checking her hair in the mirror.

"She seemed nice," Violet began.

"Who cares about nice, did you *see* her?" Lex exhaled appreciatively. "Why don't we get women like that in Harmony?" She smiled. "No offense."

"I didn't know you..."

Lex observed her in the mirror, raising an eyebrow. "That I like girls?"

"Yeah."

"Does it matter?"

"No, of course not; I just feel bad that I never asked."

Lex snorted. "You don't need to ask if someone's a lesbian when you meet them. Just like I don't need to announce it. We all just are what we are."

"Are you going to see her again?"

"No idea." She cocked her head to one side, observing Violet more intently. "Are you okay? You sound kind of tense."

"Yeah, I'm fine." She changed the subject quickly. "I saw you dancing with Joe."

"No, you saw Joe dancing *around* me. There was no way I was participating in that horror story."

"Why was he moving like that?"

"I want to say, 'childhood trauma'?" Lex grinned. "He bet me he could get more attention on the dance floor than I could. I didn't realize he was going to do it by acting like a parasite was living in his brain."

Violet smiled, but Lex held her gaze for a while longer than usual. "Are you sure you're alright?"

"Yeah, I just needed a break from the noise."

"Okay, well I'll see you later." Lex left the bathrooms, allowing Violet a few minutes to splash water on her face and try to pull herself together. Seeing Matt and Anna dancing like that was bad enough, but Anna's snide comments were an added bonus she didn't need.

"Is that the right size for you?"

Violet gritted her teeth. She'd have to try to stay out

of Anna's way for the rest of the evening. Otherwise, she might do something rash, like accidentally tear her nose off. She took a deep breath, tucking her hair behind her ears and trying to decide the minimum amount of time she would need to stay at the party before slipping out. Maybe she could pretend to be sick. Jack would understand.

Stepping out of the bathroom, she headed back down the corridor to the party but was suddenly grabbed by the arm and pulled to the side.

I swear to god, Anna—

But it wasn't Anna, it was Matt. He smiled, releasing his hold. "Hey."

"Hey." Violet's heart raced, but she kept her face bright. "Enjoying the party?"

"Oh yeah. It's a blast. Some guy just threw up on my shoes, and I had to wash them in the sink." He lowered his voice slightly as a group of laughing women passed them. "I'm sorry we haven't had a chance to talk. I was planning to find you later, but you looked upset. I was worried, so I came looking for you."

"Plus, you had vomit on your shoes."

"That, too, but let's just pretend my sole intention was finding you." He smiled again, and Violet felt her walls coming down. She wondered whether she'd been too rash inviting Jack to the party with her. Maybe things with Matt weren't so complicated after all? Then, she noticed a small dressing over one of his fingers.

"What's that?"

He followed her gaze. "Oh, Anna dropped a glass. I was helping clean it up, and I cut myself. Luckily that old lady with the eye was willing to sell me a bandage. I wanted to make sure it was covered up before we spoke."

Otherwise I might lose control and rip your arm off.

If she'd been anywhere near Matt when he'd cut himself, that tiny wound would've been all it took. She wondered how she could be so stupid to have let things get this far. She hated the fact that Anna was right, which was probably the reason her tone was so brisk when she finally spoke. "Don't be worried about me. I'm fine."

Matt looked a little taken aback. "Okay... Are you mad at me?"

"Why would I be?"

"Well, because we haven't spoken since..."

"Don't worry about it."

Now he seemed more confused than ever. "Don't worry about it?"

The words she needed to say would sting, but she forced them out anyway. "It was a mistake. I know that."

"You do?"

"Yeah. It doesn't matter."

Matt stiffened. "Where is this coming from?"

Violet forced herself to shrug like her own words didn't feel like shards of glass slicing through her veins. "We both know what it was—we just got caught up in the moment. It couldn't ever be anything else, and it's easier if we don't complicate things."

He took a step closer, reaching out. "Violet..."

She moved back, avoiding his touch. "No, we can't. I don't want to do this. I don't want you." She took a breath, barely able to meet his eye. Eventually, after what felt like a lifetime, he turned away, slowly heading back to the party.

Violet felt a bloody tear streak down her cheek. "I'm sorry," she whispered as he disappeared from view.

TWENTY-ONE

EXCELLENT JOB. THERE'S ONLY EVER BEEN ONE GUY you've really cared about, and you just sent him away.

And you made sure to talk to him like he was garbage beforehand.

Super.

Violet took a large swig of amber liquid from the glass in front of her. It burned the back of her throat, but thanks to deadened taste buds, she at least had no idea how awful it tasted. She poured another glass. Then another. Taste or not, it certainly made her head feel deliciously fuzzy with each gulp. Time slipped dreamily by, and she watched lazily as the people around her continued to enjoy the party. Joe was up on the makeshift stage now, playing the violin. Unfortunately for everyone else, it was obvious he had never so much as held the instrument in his life, and the sound he made was comparable to a cat being swung around by its tail. Luckily, the people dancing seemed to enjoy his attempts nonetheless, and the other musicians were working hard to try and drown him out.

Lex was dancing with Kiera not too far from the dark corner where Violet sat, and Toby and the other kids were sliding around the floor on their knees.

She couldn't see Matt.

"Save some for the rest of us."

189

Jack slid into the seat beside her, gently taking the glass out of her hand and sniffing the contents. He pulled a surprised face, but Violet snatched her drink back.

"S'more over there."

What's wrong with your voice?

Are you drunk?

Jack's tone was soft. "I've been looking for you for the last hour."

She didn't realize she'd been gone for that long and felt a mild stab of shame at having walked out on him in the middle of the party. "Sorry. I was here."

"I see that now. Have you been drinking alone this whole time?"

"You make it sound pathetic."

"No, I just—"

"Don't worry... 's pathetic." Tears threatened, so she distracted herself with another large gulp from her glass.

When she reached for the bottle on the table, making to refill her cup again, Jack moved it aside and got to his feet. He held out his hand. "I think that's probably enough for now."

"I'm fine," Violet murmured, but she allowed him to pull her up. She stumbled, his grip on her arm the only thing stopping her from falling face-first onto the floor. "Actually, maybe you're right."

"Let's get you home." He maneuvered her around the table and through the crowd. The pleasant fuzziness she'd been enjoying had disappeared. Now she just felt sick and as though her feet didn't belong to her. They moved past the spot where the band was performing, and Violet saw that Joe had given up the violin—or possibly had it taken away—and was talking to the man who had been playing the box-shaped drum.

"So, when did you get started playing the box?" Joe asked, a slight slur to his voice.

"It's actually called a cajón, and I started a few years ago."

"Were you, like, moving to a new house and you thought, 'I'll have a go on one of those boxes?'"

"It's not a real box, that's just the shape. It's a drum."

Joe nodded. "Right, cool, got it." He eyed the instruments. "You don't use sticks, though?"

"No, just like when you play the bongos."

"But you can't keep stuff in bongos..."

"It's not a box, man."

There was movement in the crowd, and Violet lost her balance, tripping and falling forward. Jack managed to pull her upright before her face hit the floor, and then he eased her closer to him. She was suddenly frightened. She'd never felt this uneasy on her feet before and held onto him tightly.

"Violet?"

Bleary eyed, she slowly turned her head and saw Matt standing behind her. He sounded mad, but his attention was focused on Jack.

"What's wrong with her?"

"She's drunk, Matt," came Anna's sharp reply from his left. "Come on, let's dance."

His eyes were still on Jack. "Why did you let her get like this?"

"I don't need to *let her* do anything. Violet makes her own choices," Jack replied coolly. "Anyway, I'm taking her home."

Matt moved closer. "I'll do it."

"It's fine."

"Let me take her."

Anna grabbed Matt roughly by the arm. "Jack's got it. Let him get her home so she can sleep it off."

Matt's eyes flicked to Jack once more, his voice stern. "Get her back safely."

"Yes sir," Jack muttered sarcastically as he led Violet away. She hadn't been able to say anything during their confrontation. As much as she'd wanted to tell them both that she was more than capable of getting home on her own, she was also more than a tad worried about being sick all over herself. That would probably make them doubt her abilities somewhat.

Soon they were outside, and the cool air was a welcome relief. Jack led her slowly from the warehouse, but when they were only a couple of yards away, she heard raised voices. Not far off, there was a crowd of people standing in a circle, all yelling at something in the middle. Jack, ever the soldier, instinctively moved toward the commotion, and seeing as how Violet was still relying on him to keep her upright, she had no option but to go, too.

There were two men fighting, one from Harmony and the other from Jacob's group. They punched and kicked aggressively, each trying to force the other to the ground. The voices in the crowd cheered on the man from Harmony, a farmer called Zane. There didn't seem to be anyone supporting the other guy. Zane swung a punch, hitting his opponent in the face and knocking out a tooth. It flew through the air with a spurt of blood, landing a few feet from where Violet stood.

Oh no.

There was nothing she could do. She was too drunk to move away on her own, and Jack was holding onto her tightly anyway. No one here knew her secret, and soon, the colors began to slip away from everything around her. Everything except the blood.

"Jack," Violet croaked, the word costing most of her energy.

"What's wrong?"

"Run."

WHEN VIOLET WOKE UP, EVERY INCH OF HER BODY HURT. Darkness surrounded her, and for a moment, she couldn't tell if her eyes were open or closed. The floor beneath her was hard and cold, possibly metal. Slowly, she sat up, reaching out her arms and finding herself surrounded on all sides by thin bars.

I'm in a cage.

She tried to remember anything that might explain how she got there, but her mind was foggy. She had no recollection of anything after the party.

Then an image, clear and sharp, came forward. Blood. She focused on it, fighting to remember what had happened. For a few minutes, all she could see in her mind was the blood, and then the images slowly grew, as though she were watching a movie whose picture was zooming out slowly. The crimson liquid was spurting from the neck of a man, and she was eating him, enthusiastically tearing off great chunks of flesh. All too quickly, she became aware of the coppery taste in her mouth, the flecks of skin under her fingernails.

I killed someone.

The room lit up, momentarily blinding her. She shielded her face with her arms.

"Ah, good. You're awake."

That was Ezra's voice. Violet's heart began to race, and she opened her eyes a fraction at a time, lowering her arms slowly. He was alone and strode across the large room to where the cage sat. She didn't recognize her surroundings but guessed she was above the warehouse, in the place where he lived. It was grand, with expensive-looking paintings on the walls, each surrounded by ornate gold frames. There were plush couches on either side of the room, both a deep purple. In front of the large, curtained windows was a huge, throne-like chair. The curtains were drawn, and Violet had no idea if it was day or night.

Ezra crouched in front of the cage, which she saw now was secured with a heavy padlock. He thumbed this casually as he spoke.

"My men roughed you up pretty bad, but it was the only way they could knock you out without killing you."

"What happened?" she asked in a voice no more than a croak.

Ezra grinned. "You put on a real show, that's what happened."

She knew the answer but asked the next question anyway. "Did I hurt anyone?"

"None of *my* people."

Her heart sank. "But someone else?"

"Yep, ripped him to shreds. Still, I hear he deserved it—took advantage of a lady who was disinclined to give her consent."

"I didn't mean to—"

Ezra shook his head. "Now don't you do that. Don't

act all repentant now, not when you're the coolest thing I've ever seen! You can become a drooler, then go back to normal—that's unbelievable. It's an incredible gift."

"No, it's not."

"I guess we'll have to agree to disagree."

"Why didn't they kill me?"

He sounded confused. "My men? Why would they do that?"

"Because of what I am. Why didn't they shoot me on sight?"

He grinned. "I guess you have a guardian angel."

ANNA WAS MAD AT HIM, MATT KNEW THAT. SHE HADN'T wanted to leave yet, but he just didn't feel in a partying kind of mood any more.

They were only a few steps out of the warehouse when they heard the first scream. Instinctively, Matt ran to the sound, despite Anna's pleas for him to stay back.

He saw Violet immediately. She had turned and was feeding on a man he didn't recognize in the center of a crowd. He felt like the air had been kicked out of him. Was this really happening? What could he do?

Jack was watching the scene with his mouth open. Slowly, as though there were weights on the end of his shaking hand, he raised his gun. A second passed, then five, then ten, but no shot was fired. The weapon remained pointed at the back of Violet's head as she feasted, but Jack did nothing. Matt could see, even from this distance, the sweat glistening on the soldier's forehead. Everyone watching was silent, no one daring to move while the biter in front of them continued to rip the dead man apart.

"Don't," Matt hissed when he reached Jack, wrenching the gun roughly from his grasp. Jack just stared at him, gaping like a fish.

Matt looked back at Violet. He knew they didn't have long before something distracted her from her meal. She'd see the crowd and try to attack them, too, if he didn't come up with something fast. He had to find a way to get her somewhere safe before another soldier turned up because chances were the next would have no problem putting a bullet in the back of her head.

Unfortunately, Matt's brain seemed to turn to mush, and it was all he could do to just stand and watch, along with the other helpless onlookers. Several of them had their hands over their mouths, and one or two were crying silently. They knew Violet; she'd been collecting supplies for them for months. No one wanted her shot, but as far as they understood, there was no going back.

"What the hell is going on here?" Ezra's voice boomed from their right.

Violet's head snapped up at the sound. She scrambled to her feet, running toward Ezra. Matt knew he had only one chance. He threw himself in her way and forced her to the ground. She clawed at the dirt, but he managed to keep her on her stomach.

"Shoot it," Ezra said to another of his men. "This is the last thing we need right now."

"Don't," Matt said, struggling to keep her down. "She's not one of them—she's immune."

Ezra scowled. "She doesn't seem immune to me, kid."

Violet certainly wasn't helping Matt's case much by continuing to scream furiously, still fighting to break free. She snapped her bloodied jaws with rabid aggression and hit her head against the ground over and over again.

Matt focused on Ezra, not even daring to blink. "Please, trust me. She's infected, but she's not like the others. She turns when she smells blood, but she always comes back. She's not dead."

The two soldiers next to Ezra scoffed, but the man himself wore an expression of curiosity.

"How?"

"I don't know," Matt admitted. "I don't understand how it works, but I promise I'm telling the truth. Please don't kill her." He turned his head to Anna, searching for support. For the longest time she said nothing, then sighed.

"He's right; she's only half dead. I've seen her do this and then go back to normal. Well... her version of it."

Ezra glanced down at Violet again. Matt could see

he was intrigued and continued hastily, "Why would I lie about this? I've got nothing to gain if she's really one of them."

The next few moments, while Ezra considered this, felt like the longest of Matt's life, and having to restrain a zombie while he waited did not make it any easier. Finally, Ezra spoke.

"Knock her out, but don't kill her. Let's see if lover boy is telling the truth."

The soldiers moved in and began to kick Violet repeatedly. Matt could do nothing but stay on top of her. If he moved and she got free, they'd kill her, but watching as two huge men kicked her over and over was torture. After what seemed like hours, Violet finally stopped struggling. Blood poured from her nose and bruises were already appearing on her face and arms, but she was still breathing. Matt got up slowly, and the soldiers dragged her limp body away. He went to follow, but Ezra stepped out to block his path.

"Not yet."

"Why?"

"Because I don't know if I believe you. Gotta find out if you're telling the truth first." His gaze turned cold as he locked eyes with Matt. "Remember what I do to liars, kid." He squeezed Matt's shoulder with a chilling smile, then followed his men. While Anna laced her fingers with his, Matt watched helplessly as Violet was dragged out of sight.

MATT HAD SAVED HER LIFE. HE COULD'VE BEEN KILLED, too, but he'd done it anyway. Violet wondered if there would ever be a time when she didn't owe him everything. Though as Ezra's cool eyes bored into her own, she briefly wondered if Matt had done the right thing. She got the distinct feeling that despite the fact she was still breathing, her life wasn't exactly about to return to normal.

"What's going to happen now?" she asked.

Ezra smiled. "I think we're going to become great friends."

Oh, Vi, what have you gotten yourself into?

TWENTY-TWO

VIOLET DIDN'T KNOW HOW LONG SHE'D BEEN IN THE cage for. She slept on and off and was let out at semi-regular intervals to use the bathroom. Day and night merged into one as the heavy purple curtains remained closed, and lights were switched off most of the time. She didn't know if Ezra had many 'good friends' in his life, but he certainly had a different understanding of what that title meant than she did.

If spending her days sitting in a cage in the darkness wasn't bad enough, the mealtimes were the icing on the horribly depressing cake. Ezra's men had initially brought her plates of raw meat, which she obviously hadn't eaten. This seemed to irritate them, as though she were being deliberately difficult.

"I don't eat raw meat," she had insisted for what felt like the hundredth time.

"You're one of the droolers—of course you do."

She really wished everyone would stop calling her that. It hardly conjured up a particularly attractive image. Despite her constant refusal of the food, the soldiers continued to bring the same thing over and over, and she was becoming hungrier with each waking minute. Finally, on their sixth attempt to delight her with a plate of entrails, Ezra had entered the room.

"She won't eat, boss," one of the soldiers said, waving the bloody piece of chicken in front of her face once more.

"Well, obviously," Ezra said, as if speaking to a child. "The dead ones don't eat raw chicken—or any chicken. It's gotta be a living human or nothing at all."

"Or fruit," Violet interrupted. "I eat fruit and cooked food and literally anything else a normal person eats. Actually, a sandwich would be great."

Ezra grinned. "I suppose a sandwich wouldn't be too much trouble."

From then on, his men brought regular, non-bloody food. After two solid meals, she was at least beginning to feel a bit more human, albeit a caged one.

This morning—she assumed it was morning because it had been hours since her last meal and she'd been sleeping for a while—no food arrived. While she was asleep, someone had turned the lights on, but there was no one else in the room with her now. Her stomach rumbled. She wrapped her arms around her legs, her dress still stained with dried mud and blood, and waited. Something new was going to happen today, she could feel it. She wasn't sure if she should be excited or terrified.

Finally, three soldiers entered, all armed, and made their way over to the cage. One of them unlocked it, and another pulled Violet out roughly by the arm.

"I can walk on my own," she muttered, getting to her feet uneasily. Being cooped up in the cage for so long, however, meant that her joints felt rusty, and she wobbled a little as the men led her out of the room. She wasn't being taken to the bathroom this time. Instead, they marched her farther down the hallway and into another room.

This one was even more grand than the last. The large windows were framed with heavy red drapes, pulled back to let in thick rays of sunshine. The walls were covered with paintings, and there were several fancy vases and sculptures sitting upon tables and shelves. The centerpiece of the room was a huge dining table made of highly polished dark wood surrounded by around twenty chairs. All were empty except for one. Ezra watched with great interest as Violet was brought inside.

"Good morning," he said, motioning for her to take a seat opposite him. She sat down, knowing that she didn't have much of a choice.

"Admiring my art?"

She didn't answer, and after a few seconds he simply continued. "I can't stand to see beautiful things go to waste. When we first built Harmony, I had a whole scavenging party dedicated to finding pieces like that"—he gestured to the paintings—"lest they be destroyed by a world that was rotting." He smiled, pouring Violet a glass of juice. "Did you have a good night?"

"Oh yeah, sleeping in a cage is great for your back."

His grin widened, his white teeth reminding her fleetingly of a wolf. "You can't blame me for being careful; you did tear a guy to pieces with your bare hands."

"Don't remind me."

"Who else knows about your little gift?" Ezra asked. "Other than your boyfriend?"

Violet said nothing. She wanted so badly to ask about Matt, but she was terrified to know the answer. Ezra killed people, Ezra cut out tongues, Ezra had kept her in a cage for days. What would happen to Matt for hiding this secret for so long?

Ezra's cool eyes locked with hers. "Hmm?" he prompted-ed.

"Is he okay?"

"Answer my questions and I'll answer yours."

"No one else knows about me."

"What about the girl?"

"What girl?"

"The one who stood up for the boy—the pretty one."

Oh, Anna.

"Okay, she knows, too."

He sighed. "I think you might be trying to lie to me, and you know how I feel about liars." He didn't sound too angry, though. In fact, his tone was almost playful. "Remember, you can still be of use to me without your tongue. Last chance now, does anyone else know?"

She couldn't tell him the truth, not when it could put Joe and Toby in danger. Joe in particular. If they started asking questions, or even looking at him too closely, he'd be at risk of being discovered, too. She swallowed the lump in her throat. "No. No one else knows."

Ezra was silent for a moment, then nodded. "Okay." He gestured to the plate of food in front of her—mystery meat and some fried eggs. "Eat."

"Answer my question first—is Matt alright?"

"Yes. He's fine. Eat."

Violet didn't need to be told twice and began shoveling the food into her mouth greedily.

He watched her for a moment, which she imagined was not a pleasant sight, then spoke. "Tell me about yourself."

"What do you want me to say?" she asked, speaking with her mouth full. "You know my secret."

Ezra shook his head. "Not about your gift; I want to know about *you.*"

That caught her off guard. She stopped eating, suddenly feeling a little sick. "Why?"

"I'd like to get to know you better seeing as how we're going to be working together."

"We are?"

"I'm giving you a job."

"I have a job."

Ezra snorted. "As a scavenger? That can't be earning you many points."

"I get by."

"Well, this is a big promotion, trust me."

"Do I have a choice?"

"We all have choices."

Sure, my choice to work for you on my own free will or you make *me. Great options.*

"So," Ezra continued, "why don't we start with the basics? What's your name?"

She raised an eyebrow. "You don't know my name?"

He shrugged casually. "There are a lot of people living here. I can't be expected to remember everyone. So... name?"

"Violet."

"Violet. And how long have you been with us?"

"About nine months."

"You've been a scavenger the whole time?"

"Yes."

"And what do you like?"

"What do I *like*?"

"What do you enjoy? Do you have any hobbies?"

"Other than eating people, you mean?"

Ezra laughed at that, but Violet was stalling. Why did this man want to know more about her? Surely knowing she had enjoyed video games and mild nerdiness in her previous life would be less than useless to him. Besides, she didn't want to share anything too personal. If she put her foot in it, she might accidentally give him more leverage over herself or her friends. The best option had to be silence.

He waited for a moment, then sighed. "You know, I was hoping we could be friends." He got to his feet, dabbing his mouth with a napkin. "Still, I suppose it doesn't matter. I hope you're ready for tonight."

"What's happening tonight?"

"Let's just call it a trial run." Ezra grinned, heading to the door.

Violet's heart began to race, and she got up, the chair falling over behind her. "Trial run for what? Why are you keeping me here?" she called after him. But he was gone.

"Come on," said one of the soldiers who'd been standing by the door. He pointed his gun in her direction. "Let's go."

Violet was led back to her cage and left there for hours. The lights had been turned off again, so she sat in darkness as the sounds from outside the window began to fade. It had to be after dark by now. She was starting to get cold. She'd not eaten since her hostile breakfast and also needed the bathroom really badly.

Finally, the lights were switched on, and as usual, she covered her eyes. She could hear multiple feet coming into the room, and as her eyes adjusted, she saw three soldiers. These were new ones, she didn't know any of their names but vaguely recognized their faces. They let her out of the cage and took her down the hall and into a new room.

This had to be Ezra's office. He sat at a large mahogany desk, fingers together and a bored expression on his face. In front of the desk a small, skinny man was on his knees. As Violet was brought closer, she could hear him begging for forgiveness. Ezra didn't appear to be overly moved, but he perked up when he saw Violet approaching.

"Well, well," he said, getting to his feet. "Our special guest has arrived."

The man on the floor glanced at Violet.

She didn't know him. She had a horrible feeling that was for the best.

Ezra walked around the desk, holding out his hands. "Now, Jonathan here tells me he absolutely, positively *didn't* kill one of my soldiers."

The man began to babble again. "I swear I—"

"Even though two of my own men saw him standing above the dead guy holding a bloody knife, Jonathan swears there has been some kind of misunderstanding."

"I never even—"

"And even though," Ezra said, voice booming now, "we have three people who swear blind that they *heard* Jonathan say—and I quote—'I'm gonna stab that guy for what he did,' he's still professing his innocence." He smiled, which somehow made him even scarier. "So, I thought we could find a way to get to the bottom of this before I die of boredom."

Turning back to Jonathan, he asked, "You know who this is?"

The man nodded but said nothing.

Ezra clapped him on the shoulder. "Speak up."

"Yes."

"Who is she?"

"The mutant."

Dude, I'm right here.

Ezra was still grinning. "That's right. And what does she do?"

"She eats your eyes."

Violet gasped. "I have *never*—"

Ezra held up his hands, silencing her. "Exactly. If young Violet smells or tastes blood, she loses all sense of who she is and becomes just like the dead ones. Then, when she's done, she goes back to how she was." He spoke as though this were something wonderful or poetic rather than the hideous curse she lived with.

Jonathan shifted uneasily on his knees as Ezra moved closer to him. Violet didn't see the knife until he'd already flicked it across Jonathan's arm. The man yelped in pain, instinctively clapping a hand over the wound. The cut wasn't deep, but it was enough to cause a dribble of blood to streak its way across his skin. One of the soldiers restrained Violet's arms, holding them behind her back as she began to feel dizzy.

"Now," Ezra said calmly, "it would make it a hell of a lot easier for all of us if you admitted what you did before she turns." He pointed to Violet with the tip of the bloody knife, laughing as he spoke. "Because she gets pretty damn strong the more you bleed, and I'm not sure my man over there can hold onto her for too long." He flashed his perfectly white teeth, and Jonathan's eyes flicked anxiously from Ezra, to his arm, to Violet.

"But I didn't—"

The soldier holding her took a step closer.

No, not forward, *go back!*

Everything was beginning to spin as the delicious smell filled the air. She tried not to breathe, but she knew she could only contain that part of her for so long. Jonathan was shaking his head rapidly, trying to stem the blood flowing slowly but steadily from his arm.

"Just tell him," she gasped as the soldier brought her another step closer.

"I didn't do it," Jonathan cried, unable to stop the blood trickling from between his fingers.

Ezra rolled his eyes. "That's not what you said when my guys found you." He called to a soldier across the room. "Kevin, what was it he told you?"

"I'm glad I killed him, he got what was coming to him," Kevin answered.

Oh come on, man. Just admit it!

The soldier holding on to her took another step. She wasn't fighting it any more. In fact, it felt more like he was trying to hold her back as she struggled to get closer to the bleeding man. Ezra watched with fascination.

"Isn't that something?" he asked. "All that aggression, all that power, all tied up in a little girl like that. It's almost beautiful." His words weren't making so much sense any more, and Violet felt her jaw snapping as she desperately tried to get to the delicious blood.

"Okay, I did it," Jonathan yelled suddenly. "I did it! He and I hated each other. I got drunk and we fought. I didn't mean to kill him."

Ezra sighed, as though he understood. He knelt beside Jonathan, squeezing him on the shoulder. "I'm sure you didn't." He got to his feet again, taking a step back from the kneeling man. "But you did." He nodded to the soldier holding Violet, who released his grip. She was barely aware of Ezra and his soldiers leaving the room, too busy feasting on the flesh of the man in front of her.

I'M GETTING PRETTY DAMN SICK OF WAKING UP COVERED in blood.

Violet sat up slowly, rubbing her aching head with stained hands. Flecks of dried blood sprinkled from her fingertips like glitter. Her dress was saturated now, and she smelled like death. Glancing around, she realized her cage was somewhere different. A lamp on a small table, and another on a desk, illuminated the bedroom. It was far bigger than the one she shared with Joe, containing a four-poster bed complete with drapery, a wardrobe, a desk and chair, a couch, a bookcase filled with books, a fireplace, and a large potted plant in the corner. There were two doors—one was closed, and the other was open and led to a small bathroom.

She also discovered that the cage was unlocked. She crawled over to the door, pushing it open slowly, mildly afraid it might be some kind of trick, and then climbed out. She spotted a glass of water on the desk and gulped down the contents greedily. It was part thirst, part desperation to get the disgusting, coppery taste out of her mouth.

Once the water was gone, she looked out of the window. She could just make out the courtyard below in the darkness, which confirmed she was still in the warehouse. There was no movement down there; it had to be late.

The door to the bedroom opened, and she spun around to see Ezra smiling at her.

"Great job, sweetheart," he said, holding out his hands widely, almost as if he were expecting a hug.

"Did I—"

"Kill him? Oh yeah."

She sat heavily on the bed, putting her head in her hands. Ezra muttered for his soldiers to leave and came to sit beside her.

"Don't get upset; he deserved it."

Violet shook her head silently. No one deserved to die like that.

"Come on now," he continued. "The guy *killed* someone."

"So did I. So have you. That doesn't mean he had to die."

Ezra mused on this for a moment, then continued. "Well, that's an issue for another day. In any case, I'm pleased to say you passed your trial."

Awesome.

"I know it might not seem like it now, but this is the best thing that ever happened to you." He squeezed her shoulder. "You're gonna be rolling in points, and no one's gonna give you any crap because you work for me. And... you know, you're a zombie."

"Can I go home?"

"This is your home now."

"What about my friends?"

"What about them? They'll keep doing their jobs, you'll keep doing yours."

"Will I ever get to see them?"

"Sure. You'll see them tomorrow."

Violet felt her heart lift a little. "Really?"

Ezra nodded. "Of course. That's when I introduce you to everyone properly. Things have been getting lax around here of late. Between you and me, some people are starting to question their roles in our little slice of paradise, and it's causing problems for everyone else. It's time to show them who's running the place and what happens to those who argue. We need to get back to how it should be. You're going to help me with that."

Violet's shoulders sank. That was exactly the opposite of what she was hoping for.

"CAN I WASH MY FACE?"

"No."

"I'm dirty."

"You're fine."

"I'm covered in blood."

"That's the point."

The warehouse door opened, and for a moment Violet was blinded by the dazzling sunlight. She held up her filthy, bloodstained arms to shield her eyes as two soldiers pushed her outside. She wore no restraints, but unless she wanted a bullet in the back of her head, she had no choice but to follow Ezra toward the stage.

She was being watched. The bells had been ringing for the past minute, and a huge crowd had already gathered. Everyone she passed was staring at her. Ezra stepped onto the wooden platform as the bells stopped ringing and held out his hand to help her up.

"I can do it on my own." She stumbled, which hardly surprised her, she wouldn't be Violet if she didn't lose her footing, but she made it up there without his assistance.

Ezra held up his hands in mock-fear. "Whatever you say, sweetheart, just don't hurt me." He grinned.

She didn't want to look at him, but she also couldn't bring herself to face the crowd that was still gathering around the platform, so she focused on the floor instead. There was a bloodstain directly where she was standing. There was one to her left, too, and another few to her right. That must have been where those people had lost their tongues. Or maybe they were from something else. She briefly wondered if Ezra had punished anyone else up there while she had been locked away.

There were more and more footsteps as others arrived, and she forced herself to glance up at the huge crowd gathered around the stage. It felt like there were a lot more people in Harmony now that she was standing up there in front of them all. They watched her with a range of emotions on their faces. Some appeared curious, others angry or confused. Some even wore expressions of disgust. But mostly she saw fear. Everyone was afraid of her. She wasn't surprised—not only had word spread about what she'd done, but there she was, standing on the stage next to their feared and respected leader, covered in blood and looking more like a zombie than she ever had in her life. She swallowed the lump in her throat, scanning the crowd for the people she cared about. She couldn't see any of them. Though surrounded by eyes on all sides, Violet had never felt more alone in her life.

"Friends," Ezra began, as always. "What an exciting few days we've had! Now I'm sure many of you know my friend here. Dear Violet has been a valued member of Harmony for many months. She worked in one of our fantastic scavenging groups, bringing in the food and supplies you all use every day. She helped bring new people here when she found them outside our walls, and from what I hear, she's a treasured friend to those close to her." He lowered his voice playfully. "And hey, she's easy on the eyes, right? Well, maybe not so much right now." He chuckled at his own joke.

There were a couple of other laughs, nervous blasts from those wanting to impress, but the crowd was mostly silent. Violet tried to ignore everyone else and focused on scanning the sea of faces for her friends.

She saw Lex first. Her expression was hard and impassive, but she was good at wearing a mask, and the fact that she didn't appear shocked or upset didn't really mean anything. She was holding Toby's hand tightly, which gave Violet some comfort. Toby, on the other hand, looked terrified. Not of what Violet was—he'd known about her for a long time—but of what was happening. He may have only been a child, but he wasn't stupid. He knew as well as she did that things weren't exactly on the up and up for her right now.

Ezra continued. "But a few days ago, we learned a little more about our dear, sweet, Violet."

She saw Jack next, just behind Toby. He wouldn't meet her eye, his gaze fixed on Ezra. This wasn't because Ezra was speaking; she knew he was making a conscious choice. He probably hated her for what she was. Maybe he was scared of her now, too.

"You see, Violet has a gift. What is this gift, friends?"

Ezra wanted audience participation? This was rare. After a few seconds, the people began to answer.

"She kills people!"

"She's a drooler!"

"She eats their eyes!"

Where the hell did that come from?

Ezra nodded slowly. "Yep. All true, and more."

Violet caught sight of Joe a few rows ahead and to the left of Toby. He'd been listening with a serious expression on his face, but the second he saw her watching him, he grinned, rolling his eyes at Ezra's speech as if bored. She felt the flicker of a smile play on her lips. Joe was mouthing something to her.

"It'll be okay."

She gave the slightest hint of a nod to show she understood.

Ezra stepped forward. "What we have here, friends, is a powerful tool. Violet is worth more to us than our guns, more than our biters on sticks. She's a weapon that no one will ever see coming, and let me tell you, she's deadly. But you don't have to take my word for it." He pointed back to the warehouse, and there was a collective gasp from the crowd.

Violet followed their gaze and put her hand to her mouth. The mangled corpses of the two men she'd killed had been strung up on either side of the door to Ezra's quarters. She could hear shocked whispers and even what sounded like crying, but the second Ezra held up his hand there was silence.

"Remember, friends, Violet is here to keep us safe—

safe from those who seek to do us harm from outside our walls... and from within."

Violet saw Matt and Anna. She didn't know how she'd missed them before; they were practically at the front of the crowd. Anna's expression was hard to read, her face set. She clung to Matt's hand tightly, and he certainly wasn't shaking her off. Violet forced herself to look at him. She owed him that, at least, for saving her life. He kept his eyes locked with hers. All outside noise faded into the background, and she simply focused on his green eyes.

Violet only realized their leader was done when one of the soldiers began to push her to the edge of the stage. The crowd started to disperse. As she followed Ezra back to the warehouse, a large group of kids cut across her path. One skinny boy collided with her, and she felt something roughly pressed into her hand. Immediately she closed her fingers around the scrap of paper, while the soldiers yelled at the kids to be more careful.

She let them lead her back up to her room without a struggle. Once the door closed, Violet waited until she heard their footsteps disappear down the hallway before she hurried into the bathroom, shutting the door gently behind her. She sat on the edge of the bath and unfolded the scrap of paper, reading the words over and over, until, when she closed her eyes, she could still see them imprinted on the lids.

Don't worry. I'm getting you out.

MELISSA IS A PRIMARY SCHOOL TEACHER BY DAY AND a writer by night. She grew up in a small town in the UK, and spent most of her time with her nose in a book. Her childhood was filled with R.L Stein, Jacqueline Wilson, and J.K Rowling, and they inspired her to begin creating her own worlds. She wrote the first draft of Alive? at sixteen, and has been hooked on writing ever since. Melissa is currently working on the third book in the Alive? series.

Melissa spends her free time learning how motherhood works, with her son Clark, who was born in early October. Turns out preparing for the zompocalypse is no match for sleepless nights and teething!

ACKNOWLEDGEMENTS

THERE ARE SO MANY PEOPLE, ONCE AGAIN, THAT I'D like to mention for their role in getting Still Alive? finished.

First and foremost I would like to thank my wonderful husband, David, who listened to hundreds of my ideas, politely informed me which ones were just plain awful, and always made me feel like I was doing a great job. Also to my mum, I aspire to one day be as incredible and strong as you are. Thank you for your constant love and support.

I would also like to thank Lorin, for her endless zombie knowledge, and ability to weave a 'what would you do if zombies appeared right now?' question into any situation.

Thank you to Luke and Joe for your endless suggestions for book titles. I'm not sure 'Bees?' or 'Zom-baby' will ever see the light of day, but they're certainly unique takes on the genre.

Andy and Vicki, thank you for your love and support, and for always being there to celebrate the end of a chapter with a game of Scattergories!

Finally, thank you to all the amazing ladies at Clean Teen, for being so helpful and supportive throughout every moment of the process. I feel so grateful to be part of such an amazing family.

...And a special mention for everyone who wanted the blurb to be straight. This one's for you!